CAUGHT UP IN A THUG'S LOVE

BY

DEIDRE LESHAY

CHAPTER ONE

Alexis

Oh, my God. What have I done? I thought as I paced the floor.

"Wesley, get up! Please get up," I yelled.

Dropping to my knees, there was a small puddle of blood under his body. I had to save his life. Wesley, why would you make me do this? I never wanted things to end this way. What the fuck was I going to do? Who could I call? I could not believe that I did not have any friends that were not attached to Chase, my loving husband. There was no way that I could call him, and my sister was on vacation. It looked like I would be doing this solo.

"Fuck!" I screamed.

Then, I sat on the edge of the hotel bed, freaking the fuck out as I looked down at Wesley Mayfield's lifeless body. He had been my kryptonite, my cheating partner, my lover, and my best friend. I had loved Wesley since I met him when I was a teenager. What would I do without him? My tears turned into a sob. Wesley was a well-known businessman. There was no way I could be found at the crime scene.

I could hear it now. Alexis Goodwin Manchester, crime news reporter, social media influencer, and a cheating wife, is being arrested for murdering local assumed Cartel leader and businessman. That wouldn't sound good on breaking news. Not to mention, I was married to the chief of police. That would totally embarrass Chase.

Damn, I thought, trying to get my thoughts together.

I was meeting Wesley for my weekly dose of 'get right'. Yes, I was having an affair, but I could justify it. I slept with Wesley before I met my husband, so was I really cheating? I married a stable, white man, who legally had his shit together, but there was something about sex with Wesley that made it hard to walk away.

My husband was Chase, the chief of police, a good all-American, blonde-haired, blue-eyed boy. He was my rebound from a bad relationship. Chase knew that my heart was jaded to love in the beginning. Wesley and I had dealt with each other casually in the past; I never hid that from Chase. That was why anytime he could rouse or piss Wesley off, he would do so with his authority. Why would Chase and Wesley have contact? Because Wesley's sister, Westlyn, was married to Chase's brother.

Imagine how awkward dinner parties or birthday parties were, especially after Wesley and I started having an affair. Thank God, they could keep it together for the kids. One day, Chase's brother said, "Alexis, I think you married the wrong man," in a joking manner. Wesley agreed, and I didn't say anything, which to Chase was a silent agreement. He was right to feel that way. I did feel like I married the wrong man.

Do not get me wrong, Chase was a good husband and provider, but he had major shortcomings in the bedroom. Let's just be frank. My husband had a small dick, and he barely scratched the surface. He wasn't sexually aggressive in the bedroom. He always wanted to give it to me slow and sexy, but sometimes, a girl just needed a man to throw her on the bed and fuck the life out of her and then fuck the life back in her. I wouldn't make any excuses for my cheating. However, this was how I got here. I needed something sexually that my husband couldn't offer me.

I should've had more self-control and been able to walk away from my past, but now, I needed to figure out how I could disassociate myself from this. I was sure nobody saw me walking in the hotel. I wore a long wig and sunglasses. I was used to reporting the news, not being part of it, and

Wesley being the street king and businessman he was guaranteed front coverage.

Now, how the fuck would I get him out of here? I was way too cute for jail. *Damn it. Think, Alexis, think.* All Black girls looked like me, so the first thing I needed to do was change my hairstyle. Great thing I had multiple wigs in my bag. I turned my cell phone off. I was on the other side of town the last time I made a call, so there was no way that I was being tracked on any towers. At least I hoped I was not. I couldn't explain why I would have been in this area. Thank God I got rid of that On-Star. There was really no way for anyone to know that I was here.

Oh, yeah, my fingerprints were all over the place. There were cleaning supplies in my car. I had been to the Dollar Tree earlier this week, and I was too lazy to take the shit in the house, not to mention that I had my car cleaning kit in my trunk as well. I put on my shades and held my head down as I ran to my car, which was parked on the corner and a fifteen walk, grabbed my utility tote, and went back in the room. I sprayed bleach on everything I thought that I had touched then removed the sheets from the bed, placing them in my tote. I didn't need my hair left anywhere. I had a mini vacuum in that tote, so I used it to vacuum the bed and the pillows, then around his body. A part of me wanted to cry. I loved this man, and I didn't mean to kill him. I was in love with him, but I couldn't have him telling Chase about our affair, and I couldn't allow him to stop me from getting this abortion. Our last conversation played in my head.

"Wesley, I took a pregnancy test last week, and I'm pregnant. Chase and I always use condoms whereas you and I never do."

Wesley smiled, and I began to feel like shit because my next sentence was going to cause smoke in the city.

"Wes, I love you, but I can't have this baby. I am going to get an abortion."

Wesley grabbed me by the arm, pulling me close to him.

"Alexis Nicole, it will be a cold day in hell before I let you kill my baby. This is how this is gonna work. You are going to tell your husband about us and the baby. I'm giving you twenty-four hours to tell him, or I will."

"Wesley Jamal Mayfield, you are not my boss. You don't get to tell me what I'm going to do. Get your fucking hands off me. I'm not going to ruin my marriage from infidelity. Not to mention, if I tell my husband that I'm pregnant with your baby, he'll want me to get an abortion anyways. Do you think that he's going to just let you have me?" I said, slightly raising my voice. This was a frustrating conversation, and as much as I wanted to be with Wesley, I just couldn't live the life that he lived. I didn't want to be a girlfriend.

"Alexis, you've known what I've done for years, and it's no problem when I'm spending my money on you, but I swear if you kill my baby, I will never talk to you again. I will end your fucking life, Alexis, and I love you more than life itself."

I was shocked that Wesley had just threatened me. As the words replayed in my head, they hurt more than when he said he would kill me. Then, I just picked up the knife and stabbed him, but I did not mean to kill him. Tears poured out my eyes, and I dropped to my knees. This was my one true love, my soulmate, and everybody knew that soulmate connections were not perfect. They could be pure hell, but I was made for him, and he was made for me. I just didn't want to be in the center of a world all the time.

I had to bring myself back to the present because those thoughts would have me splitting my wrist any second. I focused on cleaning up the evidence. Wesley had so many enemies that no one would ever think that I killed him. I hoped and prayed that he didn't tell anybody that I was at the hotel with him.

For the next forty-five minutes, I wiped everything and stripped down the bed. I poured the bleach cleaner on the floor and mixed it with some ammonia. Then, I reached in his pocket and took out a Black & Mild and set the room on fire as I was out the door. I ran to my car. How could I live with myself after what I had just done?

Chase

I'd been calling Alexis for hours; her phone had been going to voicemail since 11:00 this morning, and it was now after 2:00. I hoped that she was okay. I got worried after I called her on my lunch. We both had demanding jobs. I was up at four a.m.; my morning was packed with meetings. Alexis, with her job as a news reporter, had a little more flexibility, so a lot of the household responsibilities fell on her.

My thoughts went back to the first time I met her. It was a double homicide. I saw her at the crime scene. I was a lieutenant then. It was love at first sight. I loved her persistence. She wore a black fitted skirt with a white silk blouse. Her ebony eyes were like pools, and I was ready to dive into them. Her hair was styled in a bob cut.

We had our first run-in when she interviewed me about the case, but I could tell she was career driven, motivated by a broken heart. She was inviting but distant. I learned quickly it would take a lot to sway her. After our initial meeting, I decided to do my homework. I saw she had ties to my nemesis, Wesley Mayfield. About ten years ago, when I was a rookie, Wesley was a street punk, and we had some run ins. I knew I would take him down, but he was always one step ahead of me. Wesley was untouchable, and I arrested him and his brother about three times. His sister, Westlyn, married my brother and had kids. Why he would ever have kids with a piece of shit like that only God knew because I sure as hell didn't. That marriage joined our families and made me and my nemesis family.

What the hell was wrong with this picture? But anyway, Wesley, his brother, and another guy ran the Gucci Cartel and had mob tries in almost every state. I could not link the two together, but after digging deeper, I realized that Wesley and Alexis had history, a past before she even told me. I was never one to date outside my race, but something about Alexis... I had to have her as mine. The fact that she was a public figure would get her past the sneers and leers of my family and friends.

I envisioned us as a power couple. Was I lusting after this mocha goddess? Yes, I was, but I considered being persistent. I was her future; she just didn't know it in the beginning. She just viewed me as another white guy who wasn't her flavor. I had to admit I did go to extremes to make her mine. I knew she was addicted to Wesley. He didn't deserve her. I turned up the harassment on him once I knew he was my competition. Alexis and I crossed paths more with the murder rate increase in the city. After months of asking her to dinner, she finally gave in. All the while, I had my guys keeping Wesley preoccupied, so I could accomplish making her mine.

My phone rang, bringing me back to reality. I assumed that it was Alexis. Imagine my disappointment when it was a call reporting a homicide at the Hilton. I rose from my desk, stopping at my friend Elliott's desk to ask him to send a car by my house. Not hearing from Alexis had me worried out of my mind. He agreed that he would call me and let me know that she was all right. As I headed to my car, I called Alexis's job to see if she was working on a story. It wasn't like her to go the whole day without talking to me. I prayed that she was okay. Fifteen minutes later, I was at the Hilton. I went to Room 4631. It reeked of burning flesh. One of the officers on the scene said that it was Wesley Mayfield. He had really pissed someone off. The M.E., also known as medical examiner Sasha Hicks, said that she needed to examine the body before she could confirm the true cause of death. My heart leaked for joy until I realized that I was going to have to tell Alexis that her old love was dead. Damn, how would I break the news to Alexis?

Shit was about to get real. The streets would definitely seek revenge, and with the job cuts I had just faced, my force couldn't handle it.

CHAPTER TWO

Nine Months Earlier

Alexis

I walked into the Vogue Lounge. Wesley had a flock of chicks cheesing in his face. I knew he saw me, but he had to be the center of attention. I just smiled and made my way to my table.

When we were younger, attention was something that he lacked. Both of his parents were drug addicts. He didn't have the latest gear or a lot of friends in school, but those factors fueled his drive. That lack was short lived.

He was hustling to support himself and his two younger siblings. He was the oldest. When Wesley was fourteen, his parents adopted his cousin, Carlton. Eventually, Wesley, Westlyn, and Carlton were adopted by a Russian mafia head name Afon. Afon loved Wesley and Carlton's hustler spirit, so he provided them with the essentials to achieve the attention he longed for. Afon always wanted kids, but his wife had some medical condition that kept her from giving birth.

I got sidetracked. Vogue Lounge was owned by Afon and Wesley, the new head of the Gucci Cartel. It was full to the max tonight with hustlers, thirst buckets, and wannabe hitters. Wesley and I had an unspoken situation. He was every woman's perfect guy; even though he was hood, he was multi-diverse.

The first time we hung out we went rock climbing. The second date we went Salsa dancing. I knew he wasn't good for me, but I enjoyed what he offered.

Before going to the table, I stopped at the bar for a drink. Chase was meeting me here, but it would be about twenty minutes before he would arrive. I ordered my drink, and Wesley slipped up beside me, flashing his beautiful smile.

"So, is that pussy mine for tonight?" he whispered in my ear.

I smiled as my kitty purred at his comment.

"You seem to already have your hands full." I flirted back. "You're looking dapper tonight." I lusted over him in a black suit with a matching black shirt and tie. His dreads were braided back, causing his two-carat earring to almost blind me.

"You're looking quite tasty as well," he chimed.

I took in the scowls and side eyes from damn near every woman in the room as we exchanged pleasantries.

"You know how we get down. I know your situation; you know mine," Wesley assured me.

"Well, go back and entertain your groupies. You know my number." I smiled.

"Most definitely, Alexis." He smiled as he made his way back to his table. Before he left, he made sure to pay for my drink.

He thought he was so smooth with his sexy ass. As soon as he walked away, I spotted Chase coming in the bar. He was cute. He reminded me of a younger version of Keanu Reeves with deep blue eyes. He was carrying flowers. Chase always went out of his way to make my day. I smiled at him as he approached the table.

"Alexis Marie, you look like an angel. Looking at you, I lost my breath."

"Flattery will get you everywhere," I said, smiling.

Chase kissed me passionately. He knew how to make a girl hot, but he was gentle. I needed kinky, spontaneous, and rough sex. I desired a big dick, and Chase wasn't that big. But after a certain age, sex shouldn't be your main focus. I'd prefer a good stable life. I could tell when Wesley was looking our way because Chase started to kiss my neck, and he was very touchy. I swore I hated the games they played.

Wesley

That damn Alexis knew she belonged to me, not that square ass cop, Chase. I sat back as I looked at all the women that flooded my club. I could have each one hands down. I wanted the one that was getting married. *Ain't that about a bitch?* I sighed to myself. I could admit I fucked it up, chasing after worthless bitches who brought nothing to the table other than pussy and some fiyah ass head. I was constantly disrespecting her with unworthy ass women. Her favorite response to shield the pain was, "We just fucking. You're not my nigga."

I knew she was in love with me regardless of what I did. She gave me a pass, so I thought. But what I didn't know was that she had her own shit brewing that rocked my world. I remembered that shit like it was yesterday. I was chilling in the Excelsior with my crew like I always did, popping bottles, talking shit like we do. Bitches surrounded us because we owned the club. I had talked to Alexis earlier. She told me she was chilling.

I was fucked up when I saw her ass walk in hand in hand with Chase. She looked good as hell, dressed in a blue maxi dress that hugged her curves. This muthafucka was flossing what was mine. My crew didn't help it by making sure I acknowledged their asses. I rose up from my table with my 9mm tucked in my waist under my jacket. I knew I was wrong. I had done my shit to her, but for her to showcase this cracker in my face in public had my Black ass heated.

I rolled up to her table then barked, "Let me holla at you for a minute." Chase and I locked eyes. I wanted him to say something. I would've emptied my clip into his ass.

"Wesley, now isn't a good time. I'll call you later," she responded, flashing her pearly whites. I was shocked. Honestly, I expected her ass to jump to bark. Chase stared at me, and I almost made a scene, but I'd be damned if I let her ass know she hurt my feelings showing up with this fool.

"Alright, Alexis. I guess I'll get up with you later," I responded as I walked away.

The first muthafucka to make a smart-ass remark is getting one in the head, I thought as I walked away.

***

I walked around Concord Mills with some meaningless bitch, and I saw her in Camella La Vie, a fucking dress store. Her ass was trying on wedding dresses. I did what any man would do in my situation. I told my groupie to have a seat while I put Alexis's ass in check. I waltzed my ass in that store and screamed her name. She turned, looking at me with tears in her eyes. She walked over to me.

"I've been calling you for three fucking months. You can't call a nigga back?"

"Hey, Wesley, it's good to see you too. I've been great. Thank you for not asking. How are you? Still running around with silly bitches, I see."

"Why haven't you been taking my calls?" I asked her again.

"Because you were looking for bitches to fuck, and I'm the woman that you should want to marry. I won't be anyone's main choice. I want to be a man's only choice, and I get that with Chase. So, he asked me to marry him, and I accepted. He loves me."

"WHAT THE FUCK, ALEXIS? I LOVE YOU." I yelled at her.

We stood there, looking at each other, and before I knew it, I grabbed her, kissing her. She needed to know that I wanted her. She broke our kiss.

"Look, Wesley, I'm about to get married. It's too late."

"Please just have dinner with me." I pleaded, and she knew I wasn't the nigga to beg.

"Fine, you have to cook me dinner. I can't risk any of Chase's friends seeing us together."

"Fine, come over at seven p.m. sharp."

She agreed. As she walked away, I bet her ass was smiling. *She will give me that pussy tonight*, I thought as I walked out of the store. Alexis had my ass all in my feelings, wanting to kill her and that square ass cracker. I looked at my watch. It was four now, so I pulled out my phone to cancel plans I had for tonight. Thirty minutes later, I was at the house, cooking for her ass like I was some little bitch. I pulled out some Porterhouse steaks I planned to smother with mushrooms and onions with some rice pilaf. I also warmed up some Hawaiian rolls. An hour later, I plated the food minutes before seven p.m. A nigga was anxious because I knew I had to mark this pussy again to get her mind right back on my team.

I called her. "Where are you?"

"I'm coming up on the elevator now," she sighed. I made sure I was on point as I wore a grey Jordan jogger suit with the newest Kevin Durant's. I knew this Gucci Red cologne would have that pussy wetter than a river. Minutes later, she entered my spot. Alexis looked good as hell, wearing some Levi jeans with a red tee and stilettos, showing her freshly painted toes. I had to admit she had a muthafucka fucked up. I was definitely kicking myself in the ass. Hindsight was twenty-twenty.

"So, am I on the do-not-call list?" I questioned as she sat down at the table.

"Why are you tripping? We were just fucking. I moved on," she responded.

That fact that she was taking this lightly pissed me off, but I played it cool.

"So, you think this shit a joke?" I grumbled.

She just smiled. I yanked her ass up, pressing her against my bar.

"Let me the fuck go," she snapped. "Do you not know who the fuck my fiancé is?" she continued.

I unfastened her pants as I applied all my weight against her.

"I don't give a fuck who he is," I boasted as I shoved my tongue into her mouth as my fingers made their way down to her sloppy, wet pussy.

"Ooh, shit," she gasped as she started sucking my tongue.

I forcibly pulled her jeans around her ankles as I spun her around. Her ass poked out as I pulled my jogging pants down. My hard dick almost ripped through my boxers. She reached back to stroke it as I kissed her neck. I whispered in her ear as I drove my dick into her. "You missed this dick, didn't you?" I said as I plunged my dick into her waiting, wet pussy.

She moaned aloud. "Fuck, I missed this good-ass dick."

I smiled to myself. I worked this dick in her pussy like a madman. I had her pinned against the wall as her pussy juices soaked my dick. Typically, she would throw it back, but she was taking it. Her ass was so stubborn; she enjoyed the dick but tried to fight the pleasure at the same time. She took this dick today. I started to suck on her neck, and she let out a moan. I must not be deep enough, so I pulled her left leg up, changing my motion. She arched her back and moved her hips. We were back to the groove. To add more pleasure, I grabbed a handful of her hair.

"This is my pussy."

"Yes, Daddy, this is your pussy," she agreed. "Yes, it's yours," she said breathlessly.

I bet her ass wouldn't be marrying that whack ass white boy now.

CHAPTER THREE

Chase

I walked in the house at midnight, thinking I'd be greeted by my beautiful fiancé, but she wasn't there, and her phone went straight to voicemail. She must be working late as I headed to the shower. I washed, got out, and she still wasn't there. I checked the microwave and found a plate with a note.

Chase,

I'm going to hang out with an old friend. Don't wait up.

I love you,

Alexis

I warmed up my food and went to bed. Four a.m. came early. I laid there watching the clock. It was after three thirty in the morning when Alexis stumbled into the house, walking like she had hurt herself. She smelled like she had just gotten out of the shower. I knew she had been with Wesley in the back of my mind. *How could she betray me?* I thought to myself as she undressed, thinking I was sleeping. What she didn't know was her disrespect to me made Wesley and his crew enemy number one. I had invested too much time into her to let Wesley or anyone else fuck up what we had. I had let him live and get rich in my city long enough. I had my guys trailing Wesley for months now. After their tryst tonight, they would hate me with a passion, but I had to show them who was really running shit. As I dressed for work, I watched as she slept peacefully, pissed to the max that she would be so bold as to fuck Wesley and then come lay in my bed like it was all good. The more I looked at her, the madder I fucking got, knowing she had been with him, fucking him after she told me she was done with him. As I walked in the kitchen for my morning coffee, I thought to myself, *If I let her get away with this shit, she will keep trying to treat me with disrespect.* I grabbed a bowl and filled it with water and ice. As I stormed in the room, I stopped for a minute. She looked so fucking beautiful. I walked closer to the bed and dumped it on her.

"What the fuck?" escaped her lips as she abruptly awoke.

I smiled then questioned her. "You just can't leave his ass alone, can you?"

Shivering, still soaked and pissed, she sat up and lied. "Who? What the hell you talking about, Chase?"

The fact that she was willing to lie only added fuel to the fire. I moved closer as I sat on the dry side of the bed. She rose from the bed to get dressed.

"So, you're really gonna fucking lie to me," I growled.

"Chase, it's too fucking early for your insecurities," she defended.

"I fucking know. I smelled the different soap on you," I snapped.

"Chase, I expect you to know better. What you smell, ass joke, is new lotion from Bath and Body Works."

"Why are you just getting home?"

"I had dinner with Chelly, then I went to the office to work on this story, and then I planned a few posts. Mr. Insecure, please take your drama somewhere else, and if you ever throw ice cold water on me again, you will need back up." She pulled the cover off the bed then went to the guest bedroom.

A part of me felt bad, but at the same time, I trusted her. I didn't like that she lied, but I couldn't prove it. At the same time, I wanted to choke the shit out of her, no lie, but I just grabbed my coffee thermos and left.

Alexis

Damn, I thought as I got out the bed. I could not believe that I fucked Wesley last night. What the hell was I thinking, going over there? I just wanted to have an innocent dinner with him. The horrible part about all this was the sex was amazing. He always satisfied me, but he left me wanting to come back for more. My goal was to leave his ass alone, but no, I had to play right into his nest. I didn't even make his ass use protection. *Damn it, Alexis, how in the world could you be so damn stupid?* Only God knew how many nasty ass bitches his ass had been laid up with. Damn. I really needed to fix things with Chase. I never meant to hurt him, and it wasn't my plan to sleep with Wesley.

Just the thought of Wesley made my pussy wet. I wanted to feel him inside me. I wanted to kiss his lips and taste him.

Damn it, why couldn't he just do right? That was what I had to keep telling myself. Wesley would never do right by me, so there was no need to waste my time. Chase, on the other hand, was loving and loyal. I had to make this right with him. I decided to send him a text.

"Hey, babe. Look, I'm sorry. It was disrespectful for me to stay out all night, but it wasn't what you think."

"What was it then, Alexis?"

I could tell that he was still pissed. He never called me by my name. I had no idea what to tell him. I was out all-night fucking. I didn't want to lie to him, but I would try to avoid it as much as possible.

"I was out with my friends, and I lost track of time. The fresh scent you smelled was lotion; it wasn't a new soap. Babe, I love you more than anything and would never do anything to jeopardize that, babe."

"That sounds like bullshit, Alexis. So, hit me back when you learn how to tell the truth."

"Why are you dead set on me cheating? If you want me to go fuck Wesley, then fine, Chase. I will call him and go fuck him."

"Fuck you, Alexis."

"Who the fuck are you talking to? I'm not one of them sorry ass white bitches that you're used to fucking. FUCK YOU, CHASE."

In the process of trying to fix things, he just wanted to accuse me of cheating on him when he was unable to prove that shit.

I had to get ready for work, so I changed the bed then found something to wear. As I was leaving the house, as soon as I got in my car, my phone rang. I knew that Chase had got his mind right, but no, it was Wesley. I sent his ass to voicemail. I made it through the whole day and nothing from Chase at all. I just happened to be heading home. I was at the stop light and saw Chase all hugged up with some bitch. His ass was supposed to be at work. I watched them walk in her house. I made a U-turn in the middle of the street, damn near hitting three cars. I parked right behind his car. Running to her door and beating on it like a mad woman, she opened it. I burst past her, running to Chase, and punched him in the eye.

"NO WONDER YOU ARE ACCUSING ME OF CHEATING. YOU THINK THAT YOU CAN JUST FUCK THE NEXT BITCH? IS THIS WHY YOU ACCUSED ME OF CHEATING?"

Before he could reply, I punched his ass again then walked out of the house.

Wesley

Seven a.m. this morning, I got a call from the county jail. I hesitated to answer.

"Speak," I barked into the phone.

"Cuz, them narcos raided us this morning," he chimed.

"No shit, that fucking Chase," I murmured. "That white boy must have found out I fucked Alexis." I laughed to myself.

"Cuz, that pussy is not worth our money," snapped Carlton.

I wondered why Alexis hadn't called me, especially after I beat them guts up. Carlton was right; we didn't need this type of heat.

"How many did they lock up?" I questioned.

"Including me, three others from our spot on West Boulevard," he responded.

"Okay, let me hop off here and holla at Mackins Bonding about getting y'all out," I assured Carlton.

"Cuzzo, real talk. Let her go. We got too much to lose," said Carlton before we ended the call.

Was Carlton out of his fucking mind? There was no way in hell I would let her go. That white boy was trying to steal my shit, and I wouldn't let it go down like that. When this was all over, Alexis would be right next to me.

What Chase didn't know was that the little breezy, Camille, he was fucking with was a dancer in my strip club, Fantasie's. I needed to keep his chocolate loving ass distracted. Camille did just the trick. I needed her to turn his ass out, and just maybe, he would leave Alexis, or it would just give me more time with her. She just needed one more dose of this dick, and things would work themselves out.

Alexis's ass had been trying to put me on the back burner. That shit wasn't happening. I hadn't talked to her ass in two fucking weeks. I didn't know why she acted as if she didn't get the memo that she was my property.

That white boy was just borrowing her ass until I figured out what I wanted to do to get things back on track with her. I knew I loved her, but she was a public figure. I was on the opposite end of the spectrum, and I didn't want my dealings to affect her career. I would never want my dirt to damage her.

I attempted to call her; there was no answer. I sent some flowers to her job, asking her to call me.

She could make me send the goons after her ass.

Alexis

I couldn't believe his hypocrite ass cheated on me. I felt like shit after my episode with Wesley, and this muthafucka had the nerve to call me on my shit while his ass was out here tricking with these thirsty ass hoes.

I was pissed but relieved his ass was cheating. I just wanted to knock his fucking head off. I never would've thought that he was a cheater. I put his ass on a pedestal while staying away from Wesley out of respect for him. And this was the fucking thanks I got.

But what he didn't know was I would still marry his ass. Ultimately, Chase was the better choice. I just had to show him my crazy girl side. On the other hand, Wesley just got an unlimited pass to this pussy. Wesley had been calling me all morning. He just thought that I would drop everything and run when he called. Let me text his ass.

"It's not a good time, Wes."

In two hours, it needed to be a great fucking time.

I needed Wesley to calm down. Chase wanted a war with Wesley. He didn't want those types of problems. After the shit he pulled a few days ago, he better not say shit about my whereabouts or what I was doing.

31

Tears streamed down my face as I packed my overnight bag with no destination in mind. I left Wesley for cheating, so there was no way in hell I would let Chase's punk ass put me through the same shit.

Just as I was walking out the door, Chase came in. We glared at each other. I folded my arms. I really didn't want to hear what he had to say, but I knew that it was coming whether I liked it or not. Poor Chase had a black eye, but he still looked extremely sad and hurt.

"Babe, can we sit down and talk?"

"Why, Chase, to accuse me of more bullshit that you are doing and feel guilty about?"

"I'm sorry. A few of my cop buddies said that they had seen you with Wesley in the mall."

"Really, Chase, you let some outsiders sell out your future wife? Yes, I talked to him in the mall. He saw me trying on my wedding dress, and he stopped in to say hi and to talk shit to me for not fucking with him. Why didn't you just ask me about it?"

"I let my ego get the best of me. I'm sorry."

Damn, I was just as guilty as his ass, but he couldn't prove it. Now, he looked extra stupid. I bet he would work really hard to keep me.

"How long have you been fucking that stripper?"

"Once or twice but that shit didn't mean anything to me. I was there for Mike's bachelor party, and she was all over me. After a lot of drinks, I let the bitch give me head. After that, we hooked up again then last night, but we didn't fuck."

"You didn't come home last night, so where were you?"

"Okay, fine. I fucked her but only because I really thought that you were with Wesley."

I almost hit his ass for lying to me, but I managed to keep it together. There was no need for me to act crazy; the ball was in my court.

"Chase, I need to take some time to process all this. You are no better than Wesley. I left him because I thought that you were different, and I thought that you would love and honor me. I won't share the man that I love."

"I don't want you to go. Baby, I'm sorry. Can we please work this out?"

"Right now, I just need time to clear my head. I'm going to the Hilton."

Chase went to say something, but I walked out the door with tears falling down my cheeks.

CHAPTER FOUR

Chase

Alexis just left me. *What the fuck was I thinking?* I thought to myself as I sat at my desk. I never meant for Alexis to find out about Camille. I fucked up. She wasn't shit to me, just a piece of easy stripper ass. She knew I was with Alexis and played her part. I knew with us being in public it heightened our chances of getting caught. I met her at one of Wesley's clubs. She was the featured dancer. We flirted with each other the whole night, and I had to have her after she sucked the life out of me.

Don't get me wrong, Alexis was on point as far as satisfying me on all levels, but she never sucked my dick like that. I was just a man who saw an easy piece of ass.

She drew me in with her sob story; she said she was only dancing to pay for school, but after dealing with her, I later learned that was a lie. Plus, that juicy ass of hers was hypnotic. It was amazing how as I got older, my taste in women changed. Before I hit my late twenties, my flavor was blondes with big tits and a flat ass.

Alexis messed me up. She was like a chocolate goddess, and I fell prey, so there was no way some broad on a come up like Camille was about to fuck up what we had, and neither was that street thug, Wesley. I knew he told Camille to fuck me, and I would make his ass pay for that. Last night was a total setup, and my ass fell for it. I wouldn't stop until Alexis was all mine. My desk phone rang.

"So, Carlton and the rest of Wesley's goons got out?" I asked the intake sergeant.

"Yeah, Chief, they were just bonded out by Mackins Bonding."

"Fuck."

"What's wrong, Chief?"

"Nothing," I answered as I ended the call.

Damn, I was hoping that those fuck boys would spend a little time in jail or snitch on Wesley, but it was death before dishonor in the streets. I picked up the phone and dialed Alexis, but she didn't answer. Her ass sent me to voicemail. I left her a message, telling her that I was sorry, and I hoped she could find it in her to forgive me.

Wesley

I smiled as Carlton and my crew walked into the clubhouse.

"Wassup, jailbirds?" I joked as they filed in. I dapped each one up as they came past.

"What's popping, boss?" they all asked in unison.

"Glad to see my squad out of those steel cages." Carlton gave me a non-approving look like he was ready to blurt something out. I looked at him and said, "Speak on it, cuz, before you burst."

By the fact that he didn't blurt what he had to say, he was searching for the right words.

"We don't need those crackers blowing us up over you dipping into his woman's pussy," growled Carlton.

I knew he was speaking the truth, but I was addicted to Alexis and wasn't trying to hear it seeing I was just in them guts last night.

"Man, I know, but I'm Pookie when it comes to her," I joked, but I could see the seriousness in his face.

I took a toke off my blunt of Kush. Before I could lie and tell him I wouldn't deal with her, my phone rang. I excused myself to take the call. Carlton shot me a side-eye; he saw it was Alexis.

I walked away as I answered the phone. "Alexis, I have been calling you since you left my house. What the fuck is going on?"

"Wesley, it is so nice to hear from you. I'm sorry that I have a future husband who was pissed that I came home at four in the morning, smelling like fresh soap."

"Can you get out tonight? I need to see you."

"Wesley, can I ask you a question? Did you send that nasty ass stripper to fuck Chase?"

"I would never hurt you, Alexis. That was all him." I lied. Hell yeah I told her ass to fuck him. If he worried about someone else, then he couldn't focus on her ass. As a matter of fact, I told Camille's ass not to give up that easy either; she had to pull out every trick in her book to get his attention. "So, the white boy cheated on you, huh?"

"Yes, Wesley, he did."

"And you're going to stay with his ass?"

"I'm not discussing this with you."

"How long are you allowed to stay out?"

"As long as I want. I'm grown."

"Fine. See you at six and you are staying the night. It's Friday. You gotta let me cheer you up."

"I'm good and no sex, Wesley."

She knew that she would give me that pussy. I had no idea why she was playing. I burst out laughing before saying, "Don't wear any panties, okay? And meet me at the strip club."

I knew her ass liked to see the stripers just as much as I did. She agreed and then hung up. Carlton stared me down as I walked back over there.

"Wesley, let me just tell you this. If I get caught in the crossfire, I'ma shoot that bitch right between the eyes."

There was no need to respond to Carlton. If anything happened to Alexis, there was no rock he could hide under.

"I have a few cops on the payroll that will get back everything we lost. Come on, muthafuckas, we got shit to do."

Alexis

I had never been so happy to see the weekend. I was sad that I wouldn't wake up to Chase. Saturdays and Sundays were the days Chase and I spent time together. Usually, I served him breakfast in bed, wearing a thong and stilettos. Then, we made love, took a nap, a shower, and then we went out on a date. Sundays, we went to church, and then I would wash and iron his clothes. Last, we had dinner with his parents unless something came up with work. It worked for us.

On my desk was our engagement picture. As I looked at it, I started to cry. What did I do to make Chase cheat on me?

"Hey, Lexi, there was a shooting. We gotta hurry up, so we can be first on the scene," my cameraman, Michael, called.

Slowly getting up from my desk, I joined Michael, and we made our way to the car. Michael had become a good friend. We spent every moment together for work. Once we were in the car, he looked at me and said, "Spill it, and don't say 'ain't nothing wrong' because you look like shit, Wesley sent you flowers, and you haven't talked to Chase all day."

39

"Damn, we need to get yo ass a woman, so you can stay out of my fucking business." I laughed before saying, "The short version, two days ago, I had sex with Wesley. Came home at four a.m. and Chase lost it. On my way home, I saw that bastard, Chase, with a stripper. Turns out Chase has been fucking her. He met her at that party y'all went to... So, I left him."

"Damn, girl, that's crazy. Do we need to fuck up the lieutenant? How dare his ass cheat on you with yo fine ass? You need to quit playing and let me hit that," he replied, cracking up.

"If you only fucked just women."

Michael was cute as a button, a little overweight but had nice caramel skin and light brown eyes. He always had my back, and if I told him, he would beat the fuck out of Chase. He was the brother I never had, and I loved him to death. The only issue with him was he played both sides of the field. He had a live-in girlfriend, Toni, but he also had a man, Marcus. It wasn't an issue; that shit was just weird as fuck.

"Michael, I need a huge favor. I need you to follow Chase, see if he's still fucking her," I pleaded. Michael shot me the side eye, then he halfheartedly agreed.

"I told you his ass wasn't what you made him out to be. And yes, bitch, you can crash at my house. Toni won't mind looking at your sweet ass. I think she has a crush on you."

We made it to the crime scene where a thirteen-year-old boy had been shot. Some random act of violence. Lo and behold, Chase was there. He was the last person I wanted to see. My cameraman saw the look I shot his ass and smiled. Chase's eyes burned a hole in me as I did my follow-up interviews with the crime scene witnesses. He watched my every move. Every time he tried to approach me, someone distracted him. I bet that was the work of Wesley. Oh, well, fuck him. He had violated, and this pussy that he craved was off limits.

Wesley

I pulled up on the scene, knowing Chase would be there. Yeah, I was being an asshole. I wanted him to know I was still working Alexis's ass like an eight-hour graveyard shift. I saw the fear in her eyes as I appeared and the hate in his as everyone on the crime scene looked at me like I was the neighborhood superstar. My appearance was necessary.

I was Louis V down to my necklace with the Louis V emblem. I watched as Chase gawked at my red 2016 BMW coupe. I did like the other onlookers. I watched as they bagged and tagged the young bull. Damn, I wondered who the fuck shot him. Someone would pay for taking this kid's life. These streets loved no one.

I made my way to the crowd and noticed that Alexis watched my every move. I stepped towards the victim's mother so that I could embrace and console her. Every eye in the crowd seemed like it was transfixed on us. I knew her son; he was a runner for me. As I freed her from the embrace, knowing all eyes were on me, I put two stacks in her hand to cover any expenses. I told her if she needed anything else to hit me or Carlton up.

As I turned to leave, the crowd parted like the Red Sea. I smiled as I walked through the crowd. I pissed him off, making her ass crave me even more. I sat in my car as I watched Chase shoot a fuck you expression my way. I just smiled as I drove away.

I had to get things ready for Alexis. She loved lingerie, so I had one of my girls pick up one of each item in her size. I loved heels, so I had them get those too. Her ass also had a sweet tooth. She would eat snacks all damn day long. I had this bitch I fucked who owned a bakery, so she hooked a nigga up. Tonight, I would get my queen back.

I ordered flowers for her and got some ingredients for chicken and broccoli.

I texted her.

"Are we still on?"

"Yes."

"Change of location. My house."

I waited for her to respond back, talking shit, but she simply said, "Okay."

Yes, now I needed to run some errands before I could get dinner started.

CHAPTER FIVE

Chase

I see I was going to have to turn up the heat on his cocky, disrespectful ass.

The way people treated him, like he was some hood savior, knowing all the time he created the chaos, I had something for his ass. I knew he was the dick that Alexis was crying on. Her ass looked at his ass like how a fat kid looked at a fresh baked cake. I knew his punk ass pulled that whole stunt for me, but he didn't realize he was burning time with me. Earlier in my career, I took bribes from the Russians, but he had me fucked up if he thought he would keep disrespecting me.

Alexis was always beautiful, but today, she looked tired. I tried to see her a few times, and people kept asking me stupid ass questions. I missed her ass like crazy. Sadly, I had been spending time with Camille. Every time I got home, her ass was at my door, half naked, trying to suck my dick. I told her ass last night was the last fucking time. And she said okay. When I got home, her ass better not be waiting for me to get off.

***

I interviewed over twenty people that knew shit about what happened to that kid. I told one of my officers that we would need to talk to Wesley and his crew. I knew that kid was a runner for him. What type of man put innocent kids in harm's way? It was a long day. I was hungry and tired as fuck, not to mention I just wanted to go home, eat dinner, and talk to Alexis. When I got home, Camille was standing on my porch, and Alexis was pulling up.

"Fuck me," I screamed.

I walked to Alexis's car so that I could explain what was going on.

"Really, Chase?" she screamed.

"No, babe, it isn't what it looks like."

I tried to calm down Alexis when Camille strolled her ass off the porch, talking shit.

"Chase, why is this bitch here? I thought you took out the trash," Camille said with a lot of attitude.

"Did this nasty ass stripper just call me trash? Bitch, you use your pussy to make money and not your brain, but what you should do is shut your fucking mouth," yelled Alexis.

"Bitch, I won't shut my mouth. What the fuck are you going to do if I don't shut my mouth?"

45

I saw this shit happening before I could even grab Alexis. She knocked the shit out of Camille. Her body fell to the ground, and Alexis straddled her, beating the shit out of her. After a few moments, I grabbed Alexis, who then attacked me. It was a struggle trying to contain her ass, but finally, I wrestled her to the ground. She tried to kick me. I didn't want to hurt her. I just wanted her to calm the fuck down. Eventually, she did calm down.

"Get off me, Chase."

"Only if you relax."

"I'm good."

I let her up, and she hopped in her car, and she left. Damn it.

I helped Camille off the ground, and she said, "I came by to tell you that I'm pregnant." I was officially fucked.

Alexis

I couldn't believe that Chase had that bitch at my house, and she wanted to run her mouth. She had me fucked up and so did he. All I wanted to do was see him. Oh, my fucking God, I could set his ass on fire right now. I got to my hotel room and got a text from Wesley, saying to come to his house.

There was no reason to even fight it. I lost the man of my dreams to some stripper. I had to relax, so I took a nice, hot bath and drank a bottle of wine. Before I knew it, an hour had passed, and I needed to get dressed, so I could go see Wes. Once out of the bathtub, I found a form-fitting red dress. I put on a bra but no panties. I decided to have two more glasses of wine. I couldn't believe that Chase was no better than Wesley. How in the fuck did I end up falling for two sorry ass men? I thought getting a white man would be better than the Black ones that I had in my life. All men were the fucking same, and I would treat them the way they had treated women for years.

I would use them to get a nut or two. I laughed to myself. I threw my hair in a ponytail. It would be easy for Wesley to pull or play in, whatever he decided to do tonight. I called for an Uber. There was no point in me trying to drive; I had been drinking. Twenty minutes later, the Uber had arrived, and the driver was cute. He told me how he loved watching me on TV and asked me for my autograph. I gave him my number instead. He smiled from ear to ear.

Awww, I thought. A man was never that excited to be around me. I got out of the Uber, making my way to Wesley's door. While standing at the front door, the aroma of food filled my nose. I had no idea what he was cooking, but it smelled great. I knocked on the door and waited for him to open it. Instead, he yelled, "It's open." I walked in to see him stirring pots. I loved a man that could cook. He had flowers and treats sitting on the table.

"It smells great in here."

"Thank you, babe."

Instead of having a seat at the table, I hopped on the counter. I opened my legs, showing him my freshly shaved pussy. He chuckled, moved the pots off the stove, and then gave me his full attention.

"I figured that we would skip dinner and go straight to dessert," I replied.

He stepped between my legs, dropping his pants. When he was close to me, we kissed, allowing our tongues to do the forbidden tango. Our tongues made a sweet song. In that moment, I was lost in the kiss, and all I needed was to feel him inside of me. He moved from kissing my mouth to my neck. I helped him out of his pants. His dick stood at attention. He pulled my dress up so that he could enter me, and when he did, I took in a deep breath as his manhood filled my insides. A moan escaped my lips as I entered the wonderful world of passion. For the first time in years, I felt like Wesley was making love to me.

"Alexis, is this pussy mine?" Wesley whispered.

I said the thing that all women would say. "Yes." I hoped that wasn't a huge mistake.

Wesley

I sat here, watching Alexis as she lay, sleeping. What the fuck had I gotten myself into? I must admit this pussy really had me doing stupid shit. I would never go against Carlton's word for anybody, but Alexis had a nigga's head fucked up. I should've left her ass alone. It was amazing how innocent and beautiful she looked. I headed into my man cave to smoke a blunt to clear my head.

I knew Chase would do whatever it took to lock my ass up by all means, so he could have Alexis to himself. Yeah, he would give her a pass on me knocking the bottom out of that pussy because he fucked up as well. I understood where he was coming from.

Sorry, back to me. I had to put some distance between us. Alexis used me to piss Chase off, to get the fucking she deserved. It wasn't love for me; it was just to piss Chase off. We both were each other's Achilles's heel. I could take Alexis from him like he could take my freedom away from me. I heard Alexis moving around, so I made my way back to the bedroom. She was sitting in the bed, looking at her cell phone, when I came back into the room.

"Hey, sleeping beauty."

She looked up at me, giving me a soft smile that didn't really hit her eyes. She looked like she had a lot of shit on her mind. I got in the bed next to her.

"Alexis, is this real?"

"Is what real?"

"This with us or are you just using me to make Chase mad? If you are, this is a dangerous game that you are playing."

"I love you, Wes. I have loved you for as long as I can remember, but we want different things."

"Your white boy is turning up the heat on us. You need to put a stop to it before I have his ass marked."

"Wesley, the only way he will leave you alone is if I go back to him, and if I do that, then you won't have me."

"Fuck it. I will kill that cracker then."

"Let me figure out a way to handle him."

We didn't say anything else about him. I made love to her for the rest of the morning and told her to meet me back here later. She kissed me before taking a shower and leaving.

***

I sat on my couch, sipping some Cognac, puffing on some pineapple Kush. I laughed to myself, knowing Carlton would put a slug in my ass if he knew I was still fucking Alexis. Just as I was refreshing my drink, there was a knock at the door. I sat my drink down on the bar and made my way to the door. I got excited as I swung the door open to be met by Chase with his gun drawn. He rushed me with his 9mm pointed at me.

"Where the fuck is she?" he roared.

I smiled then sneered, "Would you like a drink?" Chase looked like a man possessed.

"Why are you fucking with me?" he growled as he pressed the barrel of the gun in the center of my chest.

I grabbed the barrel then grimaced. "Muthafucka, are you serious?"

Chase flinched at my response.

"You running up in my shit, looking for Alexis, pulling out your gun. Get the fuck out of here." I laughed.

The fact that I was taking him so lightly only pissed him off. He took the gun and smacked me across my face. I grabbed my face as I tasted blood in my mouth. I rushed his ass, knocking him off balance. The gun slid by the front door. I pinned his white ass down. I hit him with a flurry of jabs to his face. He winced in pain as his face was now discolored from my blows.

"Get the fuck out of my spot," I spat as I yoked his ass up by his collar.

"This shit isn't over," he yelled as I dragged his ass to the door. I slung his gun out the door. I knew he was in a bad head space. As he cleared my doorway, Alexis was pulling up. I stood in the doorway as he was trying to get his wits about him after the ass whooping, I had just laid on him.

"What the fuck are you doing here?" he yelled in Alexis's direction as he propped himself on his car.

Alexis looked in his direction, rolling her eyes. "Chase, go home to Camille. We're done."

"Chase, right now, you're trespassing. Do I need to call 911?" I teased as he watched Alexis hug me.

"This shit is not over, Wesley, believe that," he threatened.

"Chase, just leave," agreed Alexis. I held my phone in the air, play dialing 911.

"You're lucky if I don't press charges on your ass," I assured him.

His face was black and blue.

"Alexis, get your ass home, or you will regret it," he scowled.

"Would you like something to drink?" I asked Alexis as I couldn't take my eyes off how her dress looked like it was painted on her ass.

"I would love a drink."

We walked into the house, and I took out a glass. Last night, she was ready to fuck, so she didn't get to open her gifts. After I offered a glass of wine, I got her stuff from Victoria's Secret.

Alexis took the whole glass of wine to the head. I could tell that she was stressed out.

"Wes, after our talk this morning and now seeing Chase acting crazy, there is only one thing left to do. That's for me to make things right with him. We could still mess around. I just don't want you to end up in jail because of me."

I fucking hated her plan, but she was right. If I kept fucking her, Chase would arrest me. I also knew that once her mind was made up, there was no changing it.

For real, I thought that I was going to have to kill that fuck boy.

CHAPTER SIX

Chase

I hit the steering wheel out of frustration. I really fucked up. I looked in the mirror at my battered face. I dabbed a handkerchief on my busted lip, pissed that I gave Wesley the upper hand in this situation. Rash thinking wasn't a good choice. If he really wanted to be an asshole, he really could file charges on me. I literally did trespass and flashing a gun only amplified the situation. Alexis had me all kinds of fucked up. Camille's presence wasn't helping any. I had to get rid of her ass; she had become a liability. I, like her, had taken an ass whooping the other day, then she said that she was pregnant. Then, she asked to crash at my place for a few days, and I agreed.

I pulled into my driveway, aggravated, not really wanting to deal with Camille's annoying ass. I cut my headlights off and coasted into my driveway to get my thoughts together. I saw her ass peeking out of the curtains. I sighed. Yeah, it was time for her ass to go. I needed time to think. I knew that wasn't about to happen with Camille around.

Alexis had it fucked up if she thought I would let her go that easily. I would let Wesley breathe for a minute until this blew over. I got in the house, and there was no dinner done, and Camille's few items were all over my couch. I wasn't used to coming home to this shit. Alexis always had the house clean, and dinner done. A few seconds later, I lost my shit. I pulled my gun out on Camille. She started crying, begging me not to kill her, saying it was all Wesley's idea. She really was pregnant, and it could be mine, but she wasn't sure. She had sex with a few other men.

I guess I wasn't the only one playing a dirty ass game, but as soon as Alexis heard that it was a setup, she would have to forgive me.

"Look, Camille, I need you to get the hell out, and we have to have some type of blood test for that baby. I have some friends that can get that taken care of asap. If and only if it is my baby, then I will take care of the baby, but I won't take care of you. You can never approach Alexis again. Do you understand?"

"Yes, I understand, Chase."

She got her shit and left. I was so stressed out that I just laid on the couch and went to sleep. I woke up the next morning to ice water being poured on me. I hopped up, and it was Alexis. I was happy to see her ass.

"We need to talk," I said.

"That's why I'm here. I need you to leave Wesley alone. I'm willing to come back to you if you promise to leave him alone. Don't put him in jail because you're mad about me."

"He had Camille seek me out and seduce me. I'm supposed to be cool with that?"

"You stuck your dick in that bitch. You were supposed to have self fucking control. So, anytime a bitch throws you pussy, you just gonna take it? What do I mean to you, Chase? When you love someone, you don't hurt them."

"Alexis, I'm sorry. I do not know what came over me with Camille, but it's over. I only want to be with you. I miss you so much. Please come back home."

"Before I agree to come home, I want you to give me your word that you will leave Wesley alone."

Even though I would tell Alexis that I would leave Wesley alone, I wouldn't. He set me up, and I would make his ass pay, especially if Camille was pregnant. I knew that I willingly fucked her, but if he wouldn't have told her to fuck with me, none of this shit would've happened. Not to mention, I hated that Black son of bitch, and he would fall for this shit. I would just have to go about it a different way.

"Alexis, there is something that I have to tell you."

"What?" she snapped.

"Camille is pregnant."

"Wow, Chase. I'm supposed to marry you, but you have the next bitch pregnant."

"I'm sorry, babe. I really fucked up, like really, really. I'm sorry."

"Fuck this, Chase. How would you feel if I was pregnant by another man?"

She had a good point. If she told me she was pregnant with another man's baby, I'd kill him and her, and I'd get away with it too.

"Alexis, I'm sorry. Shit got out of control. I promise to make it up to you."

Alexis didn't say anything at all. She just rose and left. If she went to Wesley's house, I would put a bullet in his head.

Alexis

After leaving Chase, I needed to have a drink. I typically would go to one of Wesley's clubs but not tonight. I wasn't in the mood for his smug attitude, not to mention, I didn't want to be drinking and driving. Since I decided not to stay with Michael and Toni, I headed to the hotel. Once inside, I went straight to the bar.

As soon as I sat down, I ordered a double shot of white label Scotch and a Coke chaser. I threw back my shot followed by the Coke. I ordered another shot and some plain chicken wings.

My phone rang, and it was Mr. Cocky, also known as Wesley. Even though I wasn't in the mood to talk to him, I answered.

"Yes."

"Your white boy is in my club looking for your ass." I knew his foul ass would come looking for me but fuck him. "Throw his ass out," I fumed.

"I cannot beat his ass again. He might press charges." I laughed. "Where are you?" fumed Wesley, like he was my man.

"I'm around," I shot back. I could tell my response wasn't one he wanted to hear, but he was a big boy. He would get over it.

"That smart ass mouth is going to get you fucked up," scuffed Wesley.

I wasn't in the mood for his ass either.

"So, you called me about Chase?" I questioned him, not giving five fucks.

"For real, I know what you are going through but reel that shit in. I'm not the one."

The alcohol had kicked in, so I just ended the call as I went back to tending to my drink. These niggas had me fucked up. I wished Wesley would put hood hands on me. I would kill that son of a bitch.

Just that fast, I had drifted down memory lane, remembering my mother standing in the kitchen as my father approached her, reaching his arm all the way back, smacking her. Her frail body flew across the floor. I was ten when that happened, and I knew then that I would never turn into my mother. I would kill a muthafucka before I let him kick my ass.

Wesley

I knew her ass didn't just give me the dial tone. What the fuck? I would have to fuck her and this white boy up. As I walked back into the club, Carlton pulled me to the side.

"Yo, cuz, wassup with the narco in here? I thought you told me that you weren't fucking with Alexis anymore," inquired an agitated Carlton.

I looked at his ass sideways and then replied, "Cuz, you know he's fucking with Camille. Calm down."

Carlton knew that I had just shot him part of the truth. He just frowned and walked off.

I wasn't lying. He was fucking with Camille, although Alexis was the real reason why he was here. She must not be talking to him, and he felt the need to bring his ass out to our club, thinking she would come through. His punk ass sat over in the corner, stalking my shit like he owned it. What kept me from putting a bullet in his brain was Alexis. She would never talk to my ass again. Then again, she had let me fuck her three times. I laughed to myself as he sported the remnants of the ass whooping I gave him proudly. Finally, I took my ass to my office and texted Alexis.

"Yo ass better not hang up on me again. I'm not that white boy."

"Fuck you, Wesley."

"You have fifteen minutes to get here before I have three bullets put in his fucking head."

"Do whatever the fuck you have to do. Now leave me the fuck alone."

She was really testing my patience. I swore she must not value his life or hers. Alexis must want to get fucked up. She thought I could not get to her ass, but I always knew where to find her ass. When we used to date, I put a tracker on her phone. In the street life, one had to protect his woman, and the tracker ensured that she was all right. She never knew that it was on her phone; it was a hidden app. I linked us up, and ten minutes later, I knew exactly where to find her ass. I must put her ass in line, so she wouldn't disrespect me anymore. I grabbed my suit jacket, left Carlton a note, and left out the back door. I didn't want that white boy following me, trying to cause me problems. Just in case he put one of his pig friends on me, I cleaned out my car, making sure it was drug and gun free.

CHAPTER SEVEN

Alexis

Damn, I could not enjoy my drink with folks coming over into my space. Yes, I was on the news, but no, I didn't want you all in my face. I slid from the bar into a darkened corner to drink in peace. I had a lot going on with Wesley and Chase's punk ass. I was pissed at Wesley for setting him up but madder at Chase for taking the bait and getting a strip club whore pregnant. Nothing against her, he was responsible for his actions. The fact still stood that her ass was pregnant. Plus, Wesley thought he was slick, trying to act interested now that Chase wanted to marry me.

Sex with Wesley was amazing, and Lord knew that my body missed his touch, and now, my pussy craved him. Hell, that was the last of my issues. What in the hell was I supposed to do now? How dare Chase fuck that bitch raw, like he didn't know that she could get pregnant? I thought his ass must think I was Boo-Boo the Fool as I took my shot of Scotch to the head. Wesley was full of shit too. I knew he only wanted me just to piss Chase off. The bar was getting crowded with onlookers, so I knew I would have to take this party to my room. I was a public figure so getting white boy wasted wouldn't be a good look for me. I rose up from my corner table to exit the bar before anyone noticed me. As I was about to go out the exit, I felt a tug at my jacket. I quickly turned around, only to be face to face with Carlton.

"Hey, lady, it's been a minute," he smiled, showing his perfectly aligned pearly whites.

Caught off guard, I stammered. "Yes, it has been." I smiled because I knew Carlton was on some crazy shit.

"So, I heard you're getting married?" pried Carlton.

I paused before answering, just wanting to get to my room.

"Yeah, in the fall if God's willing." I lied as I saw three guys walk up behind him. I hurriedly said, "Well, it was nice seeing you."

But his facial expression darkened as he picked up on me trying to leave. One of the guys moved closer.

"So, your fiancé cool with you fucking my cousin?" spat Carlton.

I was speechless at his question. I responded, "Last I remembered, Wesley and I were grown," as I rolled my eyes.

"Watch your fucking mouth when it fucks with my money," fumed Carlton, now pointing at me.

Just that quick, he went from zero to messy. I started to walk away when one of the guys blocked my path.

"Excuse me please," I said, but he didn't budge.

I whipped around to face a smiling Carlton.

I rolled my eyes, now aggravated, "Can you get your goon?" But he continued to smile.

"Can you stop fucking my cousin?" he responded.

"Look, Carlton, I told Chase to leave y'all alone. I would never fuck with y'alls' money."

"Why the fuck was he looking for you in my fucking club?"

"You need to ask him that. Last time I checked, I'm not him. Or ask that stripper bitch that's pregnant with his baby. Now leave me the fuck alone."

As those words left my mouth, Wesley walked up. He noticed the uneasy look on my face.

"Lex, you good?" he questioned, looking concerned but pissed at the same time.

"Carlton wants us to stop fucking. He ruined my alone time. This is all your fault. You sent that slut after Chase, and now, Chase wants a war."

"Tony, take Alexis to her room." Wesley calmly barked at the man blocking me.

He finally spoke. "C'mon, let's go. You heard Wesley."

I looked at Wesley and sighed. "I'm a big girl. I don't need an escort."

"Alexis, can you do what the fuck I ask for once?" Wesley snapped.

Rolling my eyes, I walked away, feeling like a prisoner. I purposely stumbled to draw his attention as Wesley went to the bar. Tony shadowed me.

"Ma'am are you okay?" he asked as I caught my balance.

I answered, "Yes, I just lost my balance. That's all." I giggled.

"Oh, my God. You're Alexis on the spot," he gushed.

I threw my hands up and smiled. "Guilty as charged. Well, you have a good evening," I chimed as I saw the coast was clear.

"You as well." He smiled.

I let out a sigh of relief. Minutes later, I collapsed on my bed, shocked at Carlton. He had never said more than a few words to me in the past.

I had never been so happy to see Wesley in my life. I was still in a drinking mood, so I went to my mini bar to see what I had on hand. I grabbed the mini bottle of Hennessy, and I dropped some ice cubes in my glass. I gulped it down and let out a hearty gasp from the burn. I was looking at the bar, deciding what I would drink next, when there was a knock at the door. I sighed and grimaced my face as I made my way to the door. I looked through the peephole but didn't see anyone. So, as I turned on my heel to revisit the bar, a knocking sounded again at the door. I stormed back to the door, and this time, I snatched it open, aggravated.

"Hey, beautiful," smiled Wesley.

He wore a chocolate suit, with a blue button down, brown and blue tie, with some crocodile skinned boots. His perfectly aligned teeth almost blinded me. I was speechless that he had found out where I was. He extended his hand, holding a dozen red roses. Where the fuck did he get roses from? I damn sure didn't see them when we were at the bar.

"What are you doing here?" I whined, knowing my body was craving him. I was floored at his persistence. For him to have roses this late, I was impressed.

"So, can a brother come in?" He smirked as I smelled the fresh-cut roses.

"I hope you checked your cousin."

He pushed past me, coming into the room.

"Yeah, I did."

"Good," I said, tossing my body in the bed.

"Let's get in the Jacuzzi," he suggested.

"No, Wesley. I don't want to get in the Jacuzzi." I repeated my statement again, trying to convince myself that the statement was true.

Wesley paid no mind to what I had said. He walked into the bathroom and turned on the water.

"I'm not taking a bath with you."

Wesley turned the water off and walked back to the bed. He grabbed a fist full of my hair, forcing me towards him. As he stood behind me, I took in his scent.

"Bend over," he commanded as he helped me to bend. He pushed his dick into me. I let out a moan. He pounded himself inside me over and over. This was his way of making me submit. Everything was about control with Wesley. I was tense, but after a few moments, I threw my hips back, enjoying the pounding that he gave me. We were having a fight with our bodies, but I was losing. He pulled my hair a little harder, and I came all over his dick. Screams escaped my lips. He kept pounding, and my legs got weak and unstable. Finally, he released his seed.

"Now, let's take that bath."

This time, I complied. We got in the tub, and I laid my head on his chest, finally relaxing and remembering all the reasons why I fell in love with him to begin with.

Chase would've never fucked me into submission.

Camille

I sat here, looking at Chase's weak ass as he was drunk again. He was all fucked up over Alexis fucking Wesley blatantly. What his dumb ass didn't know was this was Wesley's baby. I ran interference for Wesley, so he could get with Alexis; he paid me well to be a distraction. Chase was a good guy when he wasn't stressed out about Alexis. But he was an asshole when he drank. When he told me I ruined his life, I responded by telling him his dick ruined his life. When I met him at his friend's bachelor party, I knew then he was lame, but the bands Wesley paid me made Chase sexy as hell to me.

Some of the bitches in here thought I was a hoe. This hoe was getting her muthafucking coins. So, I would be a hoe if I had fifteen grand in the bank, and I managed to break up a happy home while another nigga paid my bills and one bought me clothes. Why they were just shaking their asses, I was stacking my paper, so fuck all them bitches.

I learned at a young age that a fat ass would get me somewhere. My mom didn't want me, so my grandmother worked long hours. When she wasn't at work, she had me all in church. Assistant Pastor Greg took it upon himself to have his way with me. He only had to force himself on me once before I learned that it was easier to do what he wanted. Soon, I realized that since I had the pussy, I had the power. Greg went from the predator, and he became the prey. He thought that I was all in love with him when I was just using him for all the stuff he gave me. Then, I met Sam. I was sixteen, and Sam was twenty-four. He had a nice car, and he always threw money like most dope boys did. He also had a woman, but I wasn't worried about that bitch. She had to worry about me. She didn't even see me as a threat. I could see why she was so pissed when she came home to find her nigga eating my pussy. I remember that shit like it was yesterday.

She had seen us together, and he said I was just his best friend. She didn't trip. A few weeks later, he and I were talking about how his back game was strong. I said let me find out you slinging good wood. We constantly flirted, and that led to us fucking on a regular basis. Yeah, I had played second best, but it always benefited me in the long run. I could've given five fucks about his main women. I was in it for the money.

Every side bitch had a back story, and I had mine. I shook my ass for cash, but it was what the fuck it was. Eventually, I would get my man. Wesley and I had a connection. I knew he thought that he wanted Alexis. But I planned to get that bitch out of his system. I thought that I had him, but he needed a little more time to see she wasn't shit.

I had to admit that I was pissed off when he asked me to fuck Chase, but Wesley wasn't the type of man to say no to. Men like him preferred submissive women. I played the part. Once again, I was hurt when I told him that I was pregnant, and he ultimately said get rid of it. Then, he said hold off on it, so I could use it to break up Chase and Alexis. Once again, I did what I was told. Hopefully, this would be the last time he asked me to do him a favor. The pay was great, but I wasn't into white men. Plus, Chase's sex game sucked; he had little dick syndrome.

I sat at the bar, waiting for Wesley to come back to the club, but he never showed up after waiting three hours. Carlton finally sat at the bar, looking aggravated. He smelled so fucking good that I couldn't help but to take in his aroma. I gave him a smile as he ordered two double shots of Jack. As soon as the bartender sat them on the table, he took the shots to the head. He ordered two more. I took it upon myself to massage his shoulders. He was so tense.

"Carlton, do you need to release some stress?"

"Yeah, bitch, let's go to the VIP room so that you can suck my dick."

"No, thank you, Carlton. I was just gonna give you a full body massage."

He jumped up and grabbed me by the arm, pulling me to the VIP room. He dropped his pants then sat down in the chair.

"I won't ask your ass again. Suck my dick."

"Wesley wouldn't like it if I gave you head."

"Bitch, you think that nigga gives a fuck about you?"

"I know that he does."

He burst into laughter.

"He loves you so much he pimped your ass out. Do you think that he would let Alexis fuck another man? I mean, really. Where do you think he is right now?"

He killed my feelings, but I would never let him do that.

"What do I get out of sucking your dick?"

He pulled his gun out and said, "To live another day."

My feet were planted, and my body couldn't move. This may be what people meant when they said scared stiff. He waved his hand up, and another girl came in with two more drinks. As she was about to walk out, he said, "How about you bitches? Give me a show. I want some girl-on-girl action."

He had to pick one of my biggest haters to ask me to fuck.

"Carlton, I won't touch that bitch at all."

"Fine, then lay down and let the bitch eat your pussy."

I pulled off my dress, exposing my baby blue matching bra and panties set. She followed suit. We looked at each other. She wrapped her arms around me, taking off my bra. She sucked on my breast, and I had to admit that shit felt wonderful. I was into it way more than I thought I would. I whispered in her ear, and she let my breast go. I removed my panties, and we walked over to Carlton. I dropped to my knees and took his average sized dick in my mouth. I sucked him as she sucked my pussy. She hit all the right spots, giving me pleasure that no man had ever given. Damn, I couldn't believe that I really liked this bitch eating my pussy. The more she turned me on, the deeper I took his dick in my mouth. I moaned and was all into the moment. He pulled my hair, and the bitch sucked my pussy and played with my ass. As she brought me to my climax, I played with his balls, giving him all the pleasure that I was getting.

He pushed my head away when he was about to nut, only to release in my face. What a disrespectful piece of shit. He commanded that the other girl lick it off. Next, he wanted her to ride my face. I refused, which didn't work out in my favor. He smacked the shit out of me then decided that he would fuck me in the ass. Usually, I was all for anal, but he got pleasure out of hurting me. He sweetened the deal by having her eat my pussy. Tonight, pleasure was pain, and my ass enjoyed every moment of it. Finally, I let her ride my face, and her pussy had a sweet taste. I got lost in her juices, enjoying every ounce of it. I sucked her dry then got her back wet again. I loved it. After a while, she and I had all the fun, leaving Carlton out. He just came and joined in the fun.

Once we were done, I hit the shower. Taking my ass to see Chase, he didn't act happy to see the mother of his child. Once I was in the house, I flopped on the couch.

"Look, Camille, I want you to get an abortion. I can't have you, that baby, and Alexis. That baby has to go. I will pay for everything. I will give you two thousand dollars, and we become strangers. Do you understand?"

"Our baby's life is only worth two thousand dollars?"

"I don't even know if it's my baby, so let's be real. I'm being very generous," he spat.

74

"That's fucked up. But you know what? I'ma do it. Then, we will be strangers. I tell yo punk ass one thing - you will be back begging me to fuck your ass again."

"Yeah, yeah, yeah. Now, get the fuck out," he fumed.

He had already packed a couple of items I had here in a bag. Damn, he was serious. Wesley was going to be pissed off.

What Camille wouldn't do was beg a nigga to stay in her life. Not now and not ever. Fuck that white son of a bitch. Okay, yeah. I was pissed off. I dumped men. They didn't dump me. What the fuck was this? As soon as I got outside, I flattened every one of his tires. Then, I started to bust the windows out of his car. He ran outside, looking like a fucking demon. I swore his eyes were red. I hopped in my car and got the hell out of there, calling Wesley to tell him what happened. He didn't answer, but I knew he was with Alexis. I went to get a room.

But twenty minutes later, I arrived at the Hilton, crying my eyes out. I checked in, having composed myself. I knew that Chase wouldn't report the vandalism I did to his car; he didn't want anyone to know about me. I grabbed my room key. As I walked to my room, I thought of how Carlton had treated me, how his words about Wesley were nothing but the truth. I was just a pawn in his and Alexis's game.

Something like a checkmate move by him. I and this baby were expendable to Chase. If Chase thought he was done with me, he was dead wrong. Wesley's ass wasn't off the hook either; he had played me as well. Thirty minutes later, I had taken my shower. I was now stretched out across the bed, pissed at how this shit was playing out. I reached for my purse; I needed the blunt I had rolled earlier. Fucking with a muthafucka like Wesley would have a bitch pulling her tracks out. Anyway, let me handle this, and I will talk to y'all later on.

Carlton

I would be glad when Wesley realized it was always bands over bitches. He got with these hoes and lost his damn focus. He knew we had too much to lose. I would take him as a loss before I went back to being broke. We ran every block of Charlotte from North Charlotte to West Blvd. But what pissed me off was bitches who flocked to his ass like flies to shit. Yet his ass chose to chase after the one bitch who he knew he couldn't have. The fact that she was engaged to Chase, he was sacrificing the whole organization. Wesley was like a brother to me; we had always taken care of each other since we were kids. My mother had died in a car accident; his mother, Joyce, had raised me like her own. Four years older, I always covered his ass. We grew up in Dalton Village, in a government apartment off West Boulevard. I learned every facet of the dope game there.

When Wesley was sixteen, he held down the front and back hole of our hood. My Aunt Joyce was usually gone over her boyfriend, Sim's house. He turned me onto the game. Now, the nigga was gone, stuck on stupid about a bitch. I should've put a bullet in her fucking head back at the Hilton. I spared her ass because there were too many witnesses. For real, I would like to fuck that bitch once or twice. She was cute, but I needed to know what the hype was. Her pussy must be sunshine. She got two niggas ready to go to war about her ass. Yeah, Chase's white ass was a mark on my list too.

I headed to see his ass right now. I pulled up to his house, and someone did a number on a car out front. Must have been a bitch. I would never understand why bitches got mad and fucked with a man's car. But I did not understand bitches anyway. He sat on the porch. It was cold as a muthafucka out here, and his stupid ass was sitting on the porch like it was ninety degrees.

He pulled his gun and aimed it at me. I got out of the car, holding my hands up.

"Chase, I come in peace."

"Why are you here?" he asked me.

"I'm here to talk," I responded.

"Well, speak then. I'm really not in a fucking mood," he mumbled as he still had his gun pointed at me.

"We have an issue," I said. "You are fucking with me because your bitch is fucking with Wesley. So, let me tell you how this shit is going to work. There is a tracker in Alexis's car and cell phone. If you keep fucking with me, I will have someone rape and kill the bitch. You need to call off your guards before she's dead as fuck, bro," I assured him. "I spoke with Wesley, and he is going to stop fucking her. I love money, and there is no reason for us to be worked up over some pussy. I also know where Mrs. Manchester lays her head at night, so be smart."

Yes, I went to his house to threaten his bitch and his mom, and that punk didn't say shit. He called me a few moments later and told me that I had a deal. I bet he had his friends checking on mommy. I told him to hold, and I had someone shoot up the spot just to be a warning that I was not the one to fuck with.

This plan could go good or bad. My plan was for him to get the heat off us. He called right back.

"What?"

"You do not know who you are fucking with. Attack my family again and I will set all y'alls' shit on fire, feds and all. Here's the deal. Tell Alexis to come home and marry me as soon as possible. Oh, yeah, and make Camille get an abortion, and I will leave you alone," he warned. "Wesley is another story. I will definitely be getting at him," Chase assured me.

"I talked to Alexis. She said that she would leave Wesley alone to save your life. So, you have no beef with him at this time," I told Chase.

"Carlton, why should I trust you?" questioned Chase.

79

I smiled. "Because I like bands over bitches. That is the Gucci Boys' motto. Wesley violated that creed, but we will handle him," I assured Chase.

"For real, Carlton. I have no issues with you. It's Wesley that's the problem. If you don't control him, then I will put him down like a rabid dog," spat Chase.

"Dude, your beef should be with your bitch. Can't nobody steal your bitch. She had the chance to walk away and the option to keep her legs closed. She willingly fucked Wesley. She is the one who's in the relationship with you, not Wesley," I fumed. "Chase, you sure you want to go this route? I mean, it would not look good if it comes out you're having a baby by a Black stripper," I teased.

"So, is that the best that you have?" he said. It was like you could hear him smiling through the phone.

"Well, let's see how you fare, seeing the locals love Alexis." I warned him.

I heard Wesley say that Chase was image conscious, which was a good way for me to get him on my side. He thought that him being with Alexis helped him get promoted quicker.

After a few moments of consideration, Chase agreed to my deal.

"I thought you would see it my way. For the record, just like you all keep files and records of us, we're doing the same. And this call was recorded." I smirked.

Chase didn't reply, which I assumed was good. I bet the cracker never thought that a hood nigga would outsmart his ass.

"Well, it's been a pleasure doing business with you," I teased.

The line went dead. That punk ass bitch hung up on me. I laughed. Now, I had to speak with Afon before any moves were made concerning Wesley. So, for now, he got a pass.

Wesley's ass would never see me coming.

CHAPTER EIGHT

Wesley

I had made love to Alexis all night, and I woke up to Carlton blowing me up. I wanted to stay in Alexis's pussy all day, but I had to make moves. I had been distracted with this Alexis shit. Today, I had to deal with Elle; she was one of our top distributors, but lately, the figures had been coming up short.

As I got dressed, I thought about how much I hated dealing with the Italians. Lately, they had been rampaging shit ever since their boss's son, Miguel, got killed. After that, their motto had been shoot first, ask questions later. Elle was over all dope operations, and she ruled it with an iron fist.

I was dressed and peeped at Alexis lying in the bed. I admired her chocolate skin on the white sheets. Damn, my dick was getting hard. I wanted to be knee deep in her pussy, but I had to go. Walking over to her side of the bed, I kissed her cheek. She did not even move. I left her a note then rushed out the room.

As I pulled up to the security gate, the armed guard waved me in. I shook my head at how they had beefed up security. I hated being ass out by coming here solo; new faces who did not know me always rubbed me the wrong way. I got a funny vibe when Elle greeted me. She was escorted by armed guards. I watched as they cooked, weighing the cocaine that was now crack. I rubbed my hands together, thinking about the money that would be made off the dope.

Our new hybrid Kush was already getting flooded through the projects. Elle watched overhead from a balcony as I took in the operation. She watched like a mother hen over her chicks in the farmyard.

I was excited at the possibilities of the money I would make off the drug haul. My mind raced at the fact that my greed had made me take out his best friend, brother, partner in crime, Manuel, in the process. I liked how Elle ran the Gucci Empire with an iron fist.

"Are you enjoying the show?" asked Elle.

"I love how you run your business," I smiled. "So, when do you think the first shipment will hit the streets?" I inquired.

"As we speak," Elle answered dryly.

"So, we're serving them as we speak?" I asked just as dryly.

Elle's phone rang, so she stepped away. I stepped closer, so I could hear what she said.

"Hello, this is Elle," she answered.

Seconds later, she screamed. "What the fuck is going on, Ortiz? Well, only thing we got going on is processing this weight. We've had an agreement for years as always. Is it Afon's dope? We do not need that type of heat at our doorsteps. Fuck. Okay, bye."

Elle returned back to the production room as I still took in the synchronicity of the operation, not noticing Elle had returned and signaled her goons to get me. My back was turned as I felt the gun barrel in my back. My body tensed as her goons clamped my neck to escort me out of the room as Elle followed closely behind with another hired gun.

"What the fuck is going on? I don't know what the fuck y'all are trying, but I damn sho is not with it," I fumed.

"Tell me where this dope came from, Wesley. Why the fuck would you bring drama to our house?" yelled Elle.

"I know you muthafuckas better put them damn guns at ease," I said.

"So, did you think you could bring dope to our house and walk away?" asked Elle.

The tension in the room thickened quickly as the goons' grips tightened on their guns.

"I'm going to give you two minutes to start talking. After that, it's out of my control," Elle assured me.

My body tensed at the thought of being fired on. I was usually the shooter. I now was the one who had death in my eyes as one of the goons' gun was now planted at the back of my head.

"So, that's how we are going to do this?" I asked as I heard the gun cock.

Beads of sweat now covered my face. The gun exploded as it caught my earlobe, and specks of blood scattered as I felt the heat of the bullet rip my flesh. I saw the light from the gun explosion.

"So, do you really want to do this?" commanded Elle as the gunpowder smell filled the room.

Blood trickled down my neck as streams of pain filled where the chunk of ear was; blood laid on the floor.

"So, talk or the next slug will be the showstopper. Did you really think you could pull this shit off?"

My neck was covered by blood that had soaked into my collar.

"I'm going to give you one minute to come clean or else," said Elle.

I took in the room and the blood hungry goons who were itching to lay my ass down. I smiled and put my hand in surrender to lighten the tension in the room. I knew I had to think quickly as the second goon had lined up an infrared dot on my chest in a shooting stance. I put my hands up in surrender.

"I just got you a stay of execution," said Elle as she looked at me getting my ear tended to.

"No stay was needed; it was just a misunderstanding on both parts," I assured her as the nurse sewed what was left of my ear. I flinched as I responded and listened. "Okay, I need to see your man, Ortiz, when this all is said and done," I barked.

"So, you're mad at him for doing his job?" Elle asked.

"At the time, his actions were justified."

I was now looking at the nub, now a remnant of my ear. I grimaced as I did so. The goon responsible walked in. I jumped to my feet and met him head on with a jab to his eye. An upper cut lifted him off his feet. I now hovered over him with his own gun pressed against his forehead.

"Muthafucka, tell me why I shouldn't body your ass."

Elle looked as the tempo of the room had changed quickly as her bodyguard, who shot me, had returned to the room. Elle took all the action in. Her guard laid on the floor, leaking blood. I was boiling mad as I lifted him by his collar and smacked the pistol against his face, making a loud thud with every strike.

"That is enough," yelled Elle as the medic who had attended to my ear now cowered in the corner. The other guard rushed in as he heard the ruckus going on in the room.

"Muthafucka, again tell me why I shouldn't kill you." I commanded. The second guard came in with his gun drawn as he burst into the room away from the production lab. Elle waved him to put the gun down and to remove his comrade.

Five minutes later, she had cleaners taking care of the mess. I, in a defensive mode, paced back and forth at the events that had unfolded today.

"What the fuck kinda shit you all got going on here?" I yelled.

Elle was unfazed by my angered demeanor.

"I don't know if you recognized it, but I have saved your ass today. A thank you would be nice. So, calm your ass down. You would've done the same thing to protect your family." I looked at Elle with lust and desire. She did the same in a standoff.

"Let's get this money and get over the bullshit," she mumbled as she made her way out of the room, back into the production lab.

"Go home and get cleaned up. We will get together later to discuss numbers. Celebrate our partnership," stated Elle.

"You owe me a fucking shirt thanks to y'all bullshit," I barked.

"Get the fuck out of here," responded Elle jokingly.

I turned to leave to take in the view of Elle again. She wore a low-cut, form-fitting dress that made her ass look rounder. Her cleavage in the dress, plus her good push-up bra, made her tits look like a D-cup. She sported a bob cut with piercing blue eyes.

My downfall was always a nice ass and a nice set of tits, which Carlton reminded me of often in the past when I did dumb shit behind a woman.

Five minutes later, I opened the door of my car. I sat for a minute to regain my composure. After today's events, I knew I had to make moves quickly.

"I can't believe this shit is unraveling so quickly," I murmured to myself as I exited the plant.

***

Back at Alexis's room...

I finished the meal that Alexis had waiting for me when she walked up behind me and ran her hand over my freshly cut head.

"Yeah, Daddy likes that." I closed my eyes and smiled.

Alexis pulled a knife from her back and put it on the right side of my head. I felt the cold steel meshing against my temple.

"What the fuck you doing?" Alexis now had her other arm wrapped around my neck and bent over to whisper in my ear.

"Muthafucka, you better had been scoping out a job. If I find out otherwise, this knife will hack on your big ass."

I stood up with Alexis still holding onto my neck. I broke from her choke hold and said, "Are you out of your rabbit ass mind?"

I now had lifted her off her feet, pressing her against the wall. Her robe had become untied in the exchange, revealing her naked body. "I bet your big overgrown ass better put me down," she commanded as I had now hoisted her legs over my shoulders. Her pussy was directly in my face.

"I got your ass now," I joked.

She had her arms wrapped around my neck. I felt her wetness.

"I bet you better put me down," she smirked.

Knowing she loved when I manhandled her and even more when I ate the pussy, I now had her at an angle. Her hands rested on top of the mini refrigerator while I had full access to the pussy. I slowly ran my tongue over her clit, slightly sucking on it. Pussy juice trickled down my hoodie.

"That's right, baby. Eat this pussy. You know what Momma likes," she moaned.

As her nails dug into my shoulders, I now sped up the strokes as her hips gyrated at a steady pace.

"You going to make this pussy cum?" I now gently laid her on the kitchen table. It was a suite set up like a studio. As I sat down, I pushed her leg open as she laid naked, spread eagle. I slowly worked two fingers in and out of her pussy as I lightly sucked and licked her clit. Alexis yelled out.

"Oh, you Black son of a bitch, you got this pussy cumming." Her body convulsed a few times, and she collapsed. I lifted my head up, my face looking like it had been soaked in baby oil.

I just smiled and said, "You should get petty more often," as I made my way back to watch a movie.

Carlton

I called Camille's stinking ass at least seven times before that bitch answered the phone.

"Hello," she said with an attitude.

"Camille, get rid of that baby. You need to tell Alexis that you were lying, and you aren't pregnant with Chase's baby. Also, tell her that Wesley told you to sleep with him."

"Wesley will kill me."

"Bitch, I will kill you."

There was a silence on the phone. I could hear the bitch crying, acting like her ass was scared.

"Camille, I know that you have a mom and a sister. Oh, yeah, and that beautiful teenage niece, Yawnha. Oh, sweet, I wonder if she's a virgin. Maybe she would like to suck my dick. Should I ask her? Camille, should I have someone pick her up, so I can do all types of bad things to her?"

"You nasty son of a bitch."

"Camille, I'm not playing with your stupid ass. Do what the fuck I say, or you will have a front row seat to watch me fuck and kill the little bitch."

I hung up the phone.

Fear would motivate a bitch to do whatever I said. But just in case the silly bitch had second thoughts, I went to Concord High School. As soon as I spotted her, I walked up to her.

"Hey, Yawnha, I'm C. Your Aunt Camille asked me to pick you up."

"Ummm. No, thank you."

I walked closer to her, grabbed her by the arm, and said, "If you scream, I will blow your brains out."

She started to cry as she walked to the car. I felt horrible. Ha. No, I didn't. I put her in the backseat, making sure the child safety lock was on. Then, I drove to a nice, quiet spot.

Once we arrived at our location, I undressed her. Well, I just took off her shirt and pants then took pictures and sent them to Camille from a burner phone with the caption, "It's your move, bitch."

Alexis

I woke in the bed alone and with so much stuff on my mind, I still couldn't believe that Chase got that stripper pregnant. That shit pissed me the fuck off. I was a damn good woman, and his ass should be proud to have me as his wife. Why wasn't I enough?

My thoughts were interrupted by a knock on my door. Who in the hell knew I was here? I got nervous as I thought about how it could be Carlton. He really hated me for some reason. I looked out the peep hole, and it was that stripper bitch, Camille. This bitch must want her ass beat.

She stood there, staring at me. Her eyes were puffy; I could tell that she had been crying.

"Can I come in?" she asked.

"Only if you want your ass whooped again. Why the fuck are you here, bitch?"

"Look, Alexis, we got off to a bad start. I only fucked Chase because Wesley told me to. He got me pregnant and told me to pin the baby on Chase. I did it because I love him, and I thought that it would make him want me. This baby isn't Chase's."

I was speechless and furious with Wesley.

"Why are you telling me this?"

"Because Chase loves you, and he's a good man."
How in the hell could I trust this bitch?

"Are you gonna have a DNA test, just to be sure?" I
questioned.

"No, I'm having an abortion," she cried.

Suddenly, I felt bad for her. I couldn't believe that
Wesley would do that.

We talked a few more moments. Then, she left, and I
got back in bed. As I lay there, my phone went crazy. Who
was texting me? The number had an 850 area code, but it was
pictures of Wesley with a white bitch. I literally felt steam
coming out my ears. Just when I thought he had changed his
ways. Who in the hell sent these photos? I was done being
the bitch that he fucked. He better hope and pray I didn't kill
his fucking ass. Tears formed in my eyes, and steam came
out my ears.

"It is time to make up with Chase," I said as I got out
of bed and hopped in the shower. After I was clean, I sent
Chase a message, telling him we needed to chat. I threw on a
robe and ordered some lunch. Nothing fancy, just a steak and
potatoes with a fresh garden salad.

It was a good thing that I ordered two. Wesley
knocked on my door. I opened the door, shocked to see a
bandage on his ear and his shirt covered with blood. He

dashed to the shower, and I found him something to wear. I was pissed with him, but I would wait before I checked his ass. He forgot that I was crazy as hell. But tonight, this muthafucka would see. He would know not to cross me ever again. I was tired of his bullshit. Sorry son of a bitch.

After his shower, Wesley sat at the table and started to eat his food. I grabbed the biggest knife I could find, rubbed his head, and then held the knife to his throat. We exchanged some words, but he didn't admit to being with another woman. Somehow, that talk led to him eating my pussy, and I thought about how the fuck I would tell him that I was done with his ass.

I enjoyed every moment of it. Once he was done, we sat on the couch. There was no need to get dressed. I knew once I said I was done, he would try to fuck me.

"Wesley, can I ask you a question?"

"Yeah, babe, what's up?"

"Are you fucking with other women?"

"Hell, nah. This time it's just me and you."

I took my phone and threw it at his ass.

"Why did someone send me this? Pictures of you and some white bitch. That was the same shit you were wearing when you came in here. Oh, yeah, and Camille said that she was carrying your child and that you forced her to sleep with Chase."

He was speechless. His nose flared, and I could tell he was pissed.

"Wesley, I can't do this. I'm not gonna be the side chick. You play too many games, Wesley. I'm done with this shit. Please leave."

"Alexis, that white bitch is just the connect. We never fucked. I flirt because women like that shit. That's it, and that's all. And Camille's ass is a fucking liar. I swear."

I rose from the couch, taking in a few breaths.

"Wesley, there will always be someone else with you. I can't do this anymore."

"Alexis, I will never let you go."

A river of tears flowed down my face. I expected Wesley to put up a huge fight, but he didn't. He just left. I ran to the bedroom and cried. Finally, my phone rang, and it was Chase. I had totally forgotten I told him I'd meet him. Now, I was three hours late.

"Sorry, sorry, babe. I have a bad headache and fell asleep. Can you just come to the Hilton? I'm in Room 5203," I answered.

"Yeah, I'll be there. Give me twenty minutes."

I got off the phone, hopped in the shower, and threw on nice lingerie. The second shower helped me relax. Although I missed the hell out of Wesley, I knew that I couldn't continue this life.

Chase didn't miss a beat. Twenty minutes later, he was there, smiling at me with some roses. We embraced. I had missed him, but sadly, all of the emotions didn't rush back at once. All I could see was him with the stripper. But he was safe, and that was what I needed right now. He sat down, and we talked about when we would get married. We decided to just put a rush on it, so we would get married on Tuesday. Then, we would have a big party and invite our friends. Not my idea of how I wanted to get married, but hell, I didn't even want to get married given the situation and how fucked up things had been between us. Maybe it was the right thing for us to do.

We went to bed with no contact at all. We woke up the next morning and checked out of the hotel room. My mind was stuck on Wesley and how he could treat me this way. When I wasn't with Chase, I was thinking about him, and when I wasn't with Wesley, I thought about him. The connection with me and Wesley was so real. And the sex was amazing. How would I live my life not being sexually satisfied by the man I love?

CHAPTER NINE

Chase

Things were finally getting back to normal. Alexis was back at home in the bed next to me, and life was great. In just twenty-four short hours, she would be Mrs. Chase Manchester. That had a ring to it. My baby would be my wife, and man was I excited. She didn't know that I planned a party for us, so as soon as we said our I dos, she would be surprised by all of our friends. I thought it would be good because she had been kind of moping around the house, pretending as if she didn't miss Wesley. But he was out of the picture. And thank God that crazy bitch, Camille, was out of the picture too. She got rid of that baby and had a talk with Alexis on my behalf, which was perfect.

She left me alone as I planned. There was nothing standing in the way of Alexis and me being together anymore. I looked at the clock. It was midnight, and in ten short hours, I would marry the woman of my dreams. I had better get some rest. My phone began to ring just as I closed my eyes to go to night-night land. I really did not want to talk to him, but he kept calling. Finally, I answered.

"We need to talk, Chase," Carlton demanded.

"Today isn't a good day."

"This isn't optional, man. Get your ass here, or I need to come there."

"Where the fuck are you? You know I'm marrying Alexis in a few hours. I don't have time for this shit."

"Hey, listen. Don't your ass backpedal on me because I recorded our whole conversation," spat Carlton.

Fuck, these fucking monkeys were smarter than I thought. I was silent for a minute, knowing I had fucked up from making a deal with the devil.

"Chase, wassup? How are we going to handle this shit?" he growled.

I sighed, knowing I had to help his ass.

"How long can you sit on her body?" I asked.

"We need to handle this asap," he confirmed.

"I'm on my way," I sighed.

Five hours later, I woke a little bit late. It was time for me to make it down to the justice of the peace. I rose from my nap. Alexis was nowhere to be found. Where the hell was she? So, I got up, brushed my teeth, and washed my face. Picking up my cell phone, I called a couple of times, but she didn't answer. What was she doing? I looked in the kitchen, the bathroom, and on the mirror to see if she left me a message anywhere, but she hadn't.

Was this a case of the runaway bride?

Alexis

I really did not want to spend the rest of my life with Chase. I missed Wesley and everything about him, but he wasn't good for me. So, I had to move on, right? I tossed and turned for what seemed like hours. I just could not go to sleep. Finally deciding to get up, I needed to get some fresh air and a couple of drinks. In a couple hours, I would be Mrs. Chase Manchester, and it might be one of the biggest mistakes of my life. My trip ended me at Wesley's establishment. *Alexis, what are you doing here? Why are you here?* Hopefully, I could slide in, throw back two shots, get back home, and everything would be perfect. Right? Wrong. Soon as I walked in the door, Wesley's goons were on me, pulling me up to his office. He was waiting in the chair with his arms folded, acting like he was some kind of Black godfather. He looked sexy. A part of me wanted to jump all over him. But I couldn't do this. I couldn't think about Wesley that way. I would be a married woman in a few short hours.

"Alexis, what are you doing here? Did you miss me that bad?"

"This is the only place I can have a drink without people recognizing me. Here I'm just another girl."

"Alexis, we both know that you're more than just another girl."

"I'm shocked to hear you say that because to you, all I've ever been is just another girl."

"So, you came here tonight to bring his shoes to the table."

"No. I came here tonight hoping that I didn't see you and that I could have a drink, and then, I want to get back home. I'm going to be a married woman in a couple hours. I wanted some freakin' peace."

Wesley's face looked like he was about to throw up. His whole body language changed. Neither one of us said anything for a few moments. I could tell that my last statement totally caught him off guard. I felt bad that I was getting ready to move on with my life and be the number one woman in someone's life when I knew Wesley loved me, and I loved him. Why couldn't love just be enough for him to say, 'Alexis, I'm going to let all of this go for you. We could run away, get married, and live La Vida Loca.' Right? In a case like this, you either conformed to his lifestyle or walked away. He'd never change. I was too old for the women, the cars, the fast life, the drugs. I couldn't do it. My heart couldn't take it if he was dead. So, there was no need for me to keep on pretending like I was cut out for this lifestyle. A part of me wanted to rush over and hug and kiss him and tell him that I was sorry. I would always be his. But I wasn't. I did what any other girl would do.

"Wesley, I have to go. It was a horrible idea for me to come here to have a drink. I guess the next time I need a drink, I'll have to have one at home."

"Alexis, please stay a few moments and catch up. I miss you."

"It was a horrible idea for me to come here, so I just better go. The last thing I need is for your crazy cousin telling Chase that he saw me here, talking to you."

"Why would Carlton be saying anything to Chase like that?" he questioned.

"Well, I'm not a hundred percent sure why, but I know that he and Carlton talk. I've heard them plotting, so honestly, Wesley, you better watch your back. I don't think that Carlton has your best interest anymore. You were chasing too many bitches for him."

When he looked at me, his whole persona had changed. He went from sad to serious, and then, he slammed his hand on the desk.

"I can't believe Carlton would cross me like that."

I walked over to him in an effort to console him. I touched his hand and said, "Wesley, why would I lie to you about this? I one hundred percent know that Carlton has been talking to Chase. I don't know why, and I don't know the extent of their relationship, but I do know that they talk. Last night, as a matter of fact, I heard him say something about Camille, and I heard Chase say, 'I'm not going to deal with this right now.' So, here's my question. Have you seen Camille tonight? Did she work tonight? If she's dead, why is your cousin calling my future husband instead of you? That's some shit to think about."

He looked at me and from his facial expression, he knew I was telling the truth. What I said made sense. Why were Chase and Carlton having conversations? Wesley took me holding his hand as a chance to grab me up and kiss me. I pulled back. I tried to fight it, but he just kept on kissing, and finally, I was overtaken by the passion. We kissed, and the next thing I knew, his hands were exploring my body, pulling up my dress. The moisture filled my secret place as he planted kisses down my neck, making his way down to my pussy. He had his face between my legs, then he pulled my panties off, threw them on the floor, and buried his face into my pussy, sucking, licking, and flicking his tongue.

This wasn't that bad if I just let him eat my pussy. Don't let him stick it in, but the next thing I knew, my dress was over my head, and he entered me. Sweet baby Jesus, I missed him so much. I let out a moan as I wrapped my arms around him and started to work my hips. It was too late to stop now, so I went with the flow. For the first time, it honestly felt like he made love to me. He did things we never did during sex. He let his guard down and stared in my eyes, telling me how much he loved me, and he hated that he was about to lose me to another man.

The fact that he had claimed to have changed and loved me so much would typically make me want to leave Chase, but I had heard this before. I couldn't fall back.

After we were finished, we laid on the floor in each other's arms. He looked at me and said, "Alexis, I know I've done a lot of shit, and you shouldn't ever forgive me, but let me just make this one thing clear please. I love you. I've never loved anybody in my whole entire life. I always had to be the head gotta-make-money. I was taught to fuck bitches and make money. It was always different with you, Lex. This last time with you, I promised myself I wouldn't fuck this up, and I swear I've been true to you. I was fucking Camille, but that was before you. I swear I didn't get that bitch pregnant. Yeah, I did tell her to fuck Chase, but he could've said no. So, can you really be mad at me?"

Damn, Wesley made a good point. Chase should've said no.

"Wesley, what about the white bitch?" I asked.

"And for real, the white girl, I didn't fuck her. Maybe I would've, but it was only some sexual tension. I promise. I love you. Elle, the white bitch, that's all business. The bitch tried to kill me. Nothing pleasurable about it; the bitch tried to fucking kill me. That's what happened to my ear. I'm laying all my cards out on the table. I just want to be with you. I think you should marry Chase, and after two or three weeks, we run away together. Spend our life together doing all the shit that we always planned when we were kids. I'm willing to give up this life for you, Alexis. I'll get out. I just can't get out and stay here."

Man, he didn't know how long I had waited for him to say those words to me. The only problem was I wasn't sure if I could trust it. Wesley only cared about one person, and that was Wesley. So, how could I trust the words coming out of his mouth? Before I even knew it, I agreed.

"Until then, we can meet secretly, and you know that Chase will have his guys on me. It'll have to be once a week, and we'll have to be out of town."

He looked at me, smiled, and said, "I know the perfect place."

"Okay, I will email the information. I know he will be tracking my phone." I smiled.

Wesley rubbed his temples, visibly aggravated.

"Just play the good wife while I get our ducks in a row," he told me.

I loved how he always took charge. That was why Chase and Carlton were threatened by him. I was more worried about Carlton than Chase. Chase was superficial; Carlton was a money-hungry savage.

"I need you to be careful around Carlton, babe," I whined.

Wesley flashed his million-dollar smile then huffed, "I got this, babe. I know he's on some slick shit."

Carlton

"Afon, we have to handle Wesley," I fumed.

Afon looked at me with his piercing green eyes.

"Why would I bite the hand that feeds us?" joked Afon.

I was pissed that he gave Wesley's ass so much credit and never once me. Afon was a Russian nationalist who was also an interpreter for foreign businessmen. Ever since we were younger, I admired his fairness and how he always balanced his double life. He was intimidating to most, he stood six foot five, around two hundred sixty-five pounds, with blonde hair and emerald eyes. He was a former military sniper, highly decorated. He was a quiet storm.

"Also, I'm hearing he has ties to the murder of Ortiz's son," I confirmed. "We don't need that type of heat from the Italians." Afon rubbed his chin, listening intently. "I mean, we have too much to lose, boss."

Afon smiled then said, "I remember a time when you all were younger, and you would've taken a bullet for him without hesitation. What happened to those days?" smiled a reflective Afon as he swished his vodka.

"Boss, we're a multi-million-dollar operation now," I responded. "We're no longer the two ragged, unkempt, Black kids. We're men you groomed to run this empire." I could tell Afon was disappointed by my response. His demeanor changed.

His voice dropped. "I corrupted you both with the finer things in life." I paced back and forth now. "Sit your ass down," commanded Afon. "I don't agree with killing Wesley, but if that's what you feel you have to do, then do it. I guess blood isn't thicker than water. Did you ever consider getting rid of the bitch?"

Afon's expression was one of disgust as he stood to leave with his three Russian goons in tow. Damn, he was right. Maybe I should just kill the bitch.

I still needed Camille to tell me what the fuck she would do. I had that little smart mouth bitch, Yawnha, at a house with some bad friends, and it was her move. I felt like my request was simple, but these bitches were stupid. If she kept playing games, I would make her watch me kill her family. I couldn't have her fucking up my money.

I sent her ass a text, telling her that she had three days before her niece was a dead bitch.

Wesley

As I pulled up to see Afon, I saw Carlton leaving, and he seemed pissed. I could only imagine that he was plotting on my life. What did it matter in this lifestyle? It was kill or be killed. It was fucked up that I may have to kill my cousin who I thought was my brother from another mother. All because he wanted to fuck my bitch. I parked my car in front of him. He looked at me as I jumped out.

"What up?"

"I thought you'd be out chasing pussy."

"I was looking for Camille. Have you seen her?"

He looked at the ground before saying, "That cop killed her."

I was stunned. Why would Chase kill Camille? Damn, was Alexis safe? We stared at each other, not saying a word. Then, I asked, "How do you know Chase killed Camille?"

He looked at me for a moment, shocked that I asked the question.

"He told me he did."

"You fraternizing with the enemy now, Carlton?"

All I could think was that my babe was right. Carlton and Chase were working together to take me down. Damn, I thought Carlton and I were better than that.

"Nah, nothing like that. I had to get the heat off us somehow. You won't stop fucking the nigga's bitch."

"I love Alexis, so it's more than just fucking his bitch. I had her first; she belongs to me. However, she made it clear that it was over. I was just some good dick, and she's going to marry him in a couple of hours."

Carlton smiled at what he thought was my pain. I tried to give an extra sad look to make him believe it was over between Alexis and me. I needed Carlton to trust me again. If we both lost, he'd be happy, but if I got her, it would be death by Wesley.

"Well, you win some, you lose some. It's fucked up that you lost to the white boy. She got all that ass, and it's going to be bouncing on his white dick."

"Yeah, it's all good. Alexis deserves to be happy, and I cannot give her what she needs."

Carlton walked past me without replying to my comment. I could tell that he was pissed, but I had to let it go. I walked into the house, and I was greeted by my two favorite goons. They never took my weapons, but they escorted me into the meeting area. Afon sat at the table with a cup of tea. I joined him. He looked very intense as I sat down.

"Hello, Wes, for what do I owe this pleasure?"

"I'm sorry to stop by unannounced, but I need to speak with you."

"Speak."

"Carlton is working with a cop, and I think they want to kill me. Yes, it is about Alexis, but I have always done my job, so I just want to know if this is on your request."

"Hell no. I would never work with a pig, and if I wanted you dead, you would be dead. You have to handle things the way you see fit. I will not get in the middle of this shit with you and Carlton. But I will say this - watch your back."

He did not have to say any more. I knew then that Carlton was really out to get me, but why? What the fuck did I do to him?

I guess blood wasn't thicker than water.

113

CHAPTER TEN

Alexis

I waited about twenty minutes after Wesley left, and then I got in my car and headed home. My mind was deep in thought about the conversation we just had. I honestly couldn't imagine that Carlton would be pissed off because he couldn't have me. There had to be something else going on between him and Wesley. Carlton had never even said hi to me; okay, maybe that was the only thing he ever said to me. He always gave me an evil eye, looking at me like he wanted to kill me. Hell, I figured he hated me.

The sound of my cell phone startled me, and I almost jumped through the roof of my car. I looked down and saw it was Chase. He probably wondered where the heck I was, probably scared that I would stand him up. I answered the phone.

"Hey."

"Where the fuck are you?"

"I had to do some last-minute errands. I'll still meet you at the courthouse."

"Okay, just wanted to make sure I was good. Hadn't heard from you."

"Chase, can I ask you a question?"

"What's up, babe?"

"Why are you and Carlton so friendly? Tell me when did y'all become best friends? I thought he was public enemy number two."

"Can we not talk about Wesley or Carlton for once please, Alexis? Can't I just have one day?"

"No choice. We need to talk about it. I will not go down the aisle with you if I think you're plotting to kill Wesley. So, you have some explaining to do. I want to know why. I want to know what the plan is, and you're going to tell me, or you can marry yourself. This is all childish games. If you would not have been fucking Camille, we would've not had our separation."

"Are you going to just keep throwing that in my face? Yes, I fucked Camille. I made a mistake, but you had sex with Wesley too. So, what makes your sins better than mine?"

I wanted to just kill his manhood and tell him how his sex was whack and how I went back to Wesley because he knew how to give it to me like a real man. I decided against it. I really needed to know what the plan was so that I could keep Wesley safe.

I softened my tone before saying, "Chase, we're trying to make this work. I don't want any secrets between us, not anymore. I need you to be a hundred percent honest with me and tell me what's going on between you and Carlton. You can't trust him; he isn't who he appears to be."

"Do you honestly think I don't know how to judge people, Alexis? I know that he's a miserable sack of shit, but I'm already in too deep."

"Why would you get involved with him anyways?"

"Why are you asking me twenty questions like this? Alexis, we're about to get married. Let it go."

Chase had just pissed me off. Without another word, I ended the call and went to the house. Chase's car was there. A part of me hoped that his ass would be somewhere else. To my surprise, there was another car in the yard. Once out of the car, I quickly made my way to the door and heard voices.

"Man, we need to leave Wesley alone. He and Alexis are over."

"He told me that today. But I don't believe it. Plus, it will just be another bitch after her. He chases too many bitches. He has to go."

"Why would you want to kill your flesh and blood, Carlton?"

"He isn't focused on our money and fucking with that will get you killed."

Abruptly, I opened the door to the house, and Carlton glared at me. There was no need to say anything. I made my way to the bedroom, closing the door behind me. Moments later, it opened, and there stood Carlton.

"Leave."

He took three steps closer to me and grabbed me by the arm, twisting it a little.

"You just gonna marry this white boy and play my cousin. For real, bitch, you could've fucked with me."

"Chase! Chase!" I screamed.

"He went to the car. I'm not going to hurt you, Alexis. We're just talking."

Thank God Chase forced me to take all of those self-defense classes; it helped me to get away from his crazy ass.

"Carlton, you slide straight to hell," I yelled as I kneed him right in the groin, running out the bedroom and right into Chase.

"Babe, are you okay?"

Before responding to his stupid ass, I smacked the shit out of him. "You brought that crazy bastard into our life, and you better get him out. Do you understand?"

Carlton laid on the floor in our bedroom, moaning in pain. Chase just looked at me with a smirk, pissing me off. If we weren't about to be in the spotlight, he would've had a black eye. After Carlton was off the floor, I threw on my wedding dress, and we left. Imagine my surprise to see Carlton at the reception hall.

Waltzing over to Chase, who looked very perplexed, I whispered in his ear. "Why is your boyfriend here?"

"I was wondering the same thing," he replied.

Chase went to speak with Carlton, who was tossing back drinks. I went to a quiet area so that I could call Wesley.

He didn't answer, and it made me mad. How could a married woman be upset that her other man hadn't answered the phone when she called? I was about to be in Rome for two weeks; hopefully, I could see him before we left.

Wesley

Damn was the only thing I could think as I watched the love of my life marry another man. Yes, I showed up at the courthouse, peeping in like a lost puppy. Hell, a nigga even shed a few tears. My Alexis didn't even look happy. Yes, she was beautiful as ever, but she was miserable. After the wedding, I needed a fucking drink. Ten shots later, I was at my crib, passed out. I woke up at two a.m. to Alexis throwing ice cold water on me. As much as I wanted to be upset, I couldn't. It was a pleasure just seeing her chocolate ass.

"Damn, baby, what the fuck is wrong with you?"

"Do you know that I have been calling your ass for hours? You fucking had me worried sick about you."

She was cursing my ass out, looking sexy as fuck in short black lingerie with matching heels. I grabbed her up and kissed her. She wrapped her arms around me, breaking the kiss and putting her head on my chest. I squeezed her, feeling her tears on my shirt.

"Baby, I'm sorry. I didn't mean to worry you. I was just sad that you had married Chase, so I got drunk."

"You can't just get drunk and pass out, babe. Your cousin is trying to kill you. He wants Chase to help him. He was at the house, then he was at the wedding and the reception. He is trying to catch us lying. He snatched me up yesterday."

"He did what?"

"Yes, babe, twisted my arm behind my back, only hurting enough to get my attention. Told me that I should've gotten with him. You can't handle him right now. If you do, he will know that we were together."

She made a great point, but I wanted to put a bullet in his head. Every dog had his day, and Carlton's day was coming soon.

"How much time do you have?" I questioned her.

"Chase got called into work. He has to finish some things before we leave for Rome next week."

"How long are y'all going to be in Rome?"

"Two weeks."

"That's too fucking long. Alexis, what the fuck am I supposed to do for two weeks without my chocolate drop?"

"Come up with a plan to get rid of Carlton. I think we can use me as bait."

I shot her a dirty look and kissed her, my way of changing the subject. We kissed a while, staring into each other's eyes, and for a moment, I just wanted to run away with her. Just wanted to keep her to myself and not send her back to Chase. She straddled me, which was perfect. I got to make love to the bride, and I planned on putting in extra work. She wouldn't be making love to her husband tonight.

Suddenly, she jumped up and made a mad dash to the restroom. I heard her throwing up.

"Babe, are you okay?"

"Yeah, I must have food poisoning."

Seven minutes later, she was back, standing in front of me, naked. Her breasts stared at me, her nipples hard. She was the perfect painting. A part of me wanted to admire her beauty, and the other part needed to be inside her.

"Are you just going to look at me?"

Alexis made her way to the bed. She attempted to straddle me, but I wanted to taste her sweet juices. As soon as she was on the bed, I went out for dinner. I ate her pussy, making her cum back-to-back. She begged me to stop, and I did for five seconds, telling her that she shouldn't taste so good. An hour later, I finally entered her, giving her slow strokes. She was wet. Don't get me wrong, she was always wet, but tonight, there was something different about her and the way she reacted to my touch. We spent the rest of the time enjoying each other.

Damn, I loved the hell out of this woman.

CHAPTER ELEVEN

Alexis

I was so sure that Wesley was back to his old tricks. I expected to find his ass booed up with some bitch. I was ready to cut his ass, and he was just passed out. Finally, he was making the effort that I was, and I was so happy. For the first time, I felt like he loved me, and he made love to me all night and all morning. It was fucked up that I spent my wedding night making love to another man. But shit happened.

I woke to breakfast in bed followed by a kiss on the cheek. "Who in the hell was this man and what the fuck did he do with Wes?" I teased, smiling from ear to ear. I took a sip of the orange juice and had to run to the bathroom and throw up. This was the second time this happened. What the fuck was going on with me? I got back in the bed.

"Babe, you okay?"

"Yes, I must be getting some stomach bug."

"I have some runs to make. For the record, I want to see you as much as possible before you leave. Make that happen."

Shaking my head to let him know that was doable, my focus was on the last time I had a cycle.

Damn, I thought I was pregnant. As soon as Wes left, I jumped my ass out of bed and went to the drug store, grabbing a few home pregnancy tests. When I got back to the apartment, I was happy to find Chase not home, and it appeared that he hadn't been there all night.

First thing first, a hot bath called my name. My private area needed a soak because a bitch was sore as fuck from Wesley. Why did his dick have to be so fucking big? While in the tub, I attempted to come up with a plan.

It had been about eight months, and for the last five, Wesley and I had been having sex and not using protection. So, if these tests come back positive, things just got complicated.

Once my bath was over, I peed on the stick and all seven tests came back positive. Damn, what the fuck was I supposed to do now?

Shit just couldn't be easy for Alexis. A part of me always wanted to carry Wes's baby, but this shit looked super bad. Married to one, pregnant by the next.

Damn was the only thought pressing my head. Should I at least tell Wesley? After composing myself, I finally got ready for work, and while I was on the way there, I stopped back at the drug store to get some stuff for my upset stomach.

To my surprise, there was Camille. I had no intention on talking to her, but she approached me.

"Hey, can we chat?"

"Why?"

"I need to get the hell away from here, and I think that you are the person to help me."

"You fucked my man. Both of you tried to ruin my relationship with Chase, and you want me to help you?"

"Look, Alexis, I'm sorry, but I did what I was told to do."

"Now, I'm telling you to get out of my face."

I walked away from her. The nerve of this bitch to ask me for help after she tried to destroy me. She was lucky that I didn't let the hood come out and beat her ass in this store. By the time I made it to work, Chase was blowing up my phone.

"Yes, Chase." I answered.

"Where are you?"

"Work."

"Sorry I didn't make it home last night. I fell asleep working on this missing teen story. I may need your help."

"With what?"

"A sixteen-year-old was taken from her school a few days ago, and I may need some media coverage. A school full of people and no one saw anything. One thing though. This is Camille's niece."

"Are you still fucking that bitch? When is y'alls' baby due, Chase?"

"Alexis, I'm the fucking police. I have to help people."

"Fuck you, Chase," I said, hanging up on him.

He called back, but I decided to turn my phone off. He had me fucked up if he thought I would help his bitch out.

Camille

My phone went off, and I got a picture of what appeared to be my niece, Yawnha. Immediately, I called her, and her phone went to voicemail, and my heart raced. I called my sister, and she said that Yawnha was at school, and it was normal for her not to answer.

Since the message came from Carlton, I decided I better call him. After one hundred times, he didn't answer. All he did was send a picture of my niece, tied and beaten. Who the fuck did that to a kid? What type of monster was he? I really didn't want to get an abortion. But I would do whatever it took to get my niece back.

I replied to the message, telling him that he won. I would get rid of my baby, even though that wasn't the plan at all. I had a friend who was pregnant, and I could change the paperwork so that he thought that I got the abortion. Then, I would leave for a few months, have my baby, then make all their asses pay for crossing me.

That was on Friday, and it was now a week later on Friday again, and I still hadn't heard from Carlton. I hated having to watch my family go crazy because our baby was missing. I got in touch with Chase, and I asked him to help me, but I knew that he was working with Carlton. He acted concerned, like he didn't know. I showed him the proof that I had an abortion, and he was happy, so happy that he let me give his ass head, but I recorded it this time. As soon as I finished, he told me that he married Alexis. That meant Wesley was lonely.

Maybe he and I could come together, and he could stop talking about being with Alexis. I called him, but it went straight to voicemail. I had a huge headache, so I walked in the store, and there was Alexis. I thought she was pretty, and after that threesome the other day, I craved pussy. I never imagined that I would want to be with a woman, but lately, all I thought about was tasting some pussy. From what I heard, she must have good pussy; all these men tried to get a taste.

I smiled at her, but she wasn't feeling me at all. I decided to say hi and ask for her help. It didn't go the way I planned. She was pissed that I fucked Chase and Wesley. I should've told her that I was still sucking Chase's dick. Soon enough, she would find out.

If something happened to my Yawnha, all hell would break loose.

Chase

Finally marrying the woman of my dreams and I spent my wedding night getting head from some stripper. Why in the hell couldn't I shake this addiction to Camille? Her head was fire; that was why. When Alexis and I got to Rome, I would tell her that she needed to better her head game. After that, I would be good. It was the only thing missing. Oh, well, for the last few months, we hadn't had much sex. Tonight, she would have to give me some ass. But hell, we couldn't get along.

Damn, did we marry for the right reason? No matter what, I would make my marriage work. Wesley didn't get the prize. I loved Alexis, and we looked good together, but were looks everything?

It was fucked up for me to ask Alexis to help Camille. That was stupid as hell. In the last five months, I had fallen in love with a stripper and gotten involved with drug dealers. Hell, I was one step away from being a bad officer. I guess I had better get this money. I had been intercepting drug deals so that the supplier wouldn't trust Wesley anymore. What Carlton failed to realize was that it looked bad on his ass as well; they were a team, and if one part fell short, the whole fucking team was fucked up for real.

***

I had to work with Carlton for two fucking hours. All I wanted to do was get home to my wife, who was pissed with me. She said that she would be hanging with Michael. I wanted to have a romantic evening, but it looked like we had to save that for Rome. Thank God we were leaving tomorrow. I got home, and Alexis was nowhere to be found. Damn, where the fuck was she? I got in the shower and went into the bedroom, noticing that our bags weren't packed.

In an effort to keep things running smooth, I packed up our clothes. Alexis had bought a new wardrobe for the trip, so it was easy. Just as I was about to call Alexis, the front door opened. She walked in, looking beautiful. She wore a form-fitting strapless black dress, some silver earrings, a matching silver purse, and matching shoes. She smiled at me and headed to the bathroom. Without a word, I followed her. As soon as she turned around to see me, I grabbed her, kissing her passionately and trying to undress her.

"Not tonight, Chase. I need to pack our stuff, and it has been a long day."

"Babe, we just got married, and I want to make love to my wife. Is that too much to ask?" I yelled.

129

She dropped the dress to the floor, exposing her naked body. She grabbed me by the hand, forcing me to the bed.

Once naked, she rode me, doing all types of things that she had never done before, forcing me to release in ten minutes flat. Alexis got off me and made her way to the bathroom to shower.

Thirty minutes later, Alexis was back in the room. She smiled when she noticed that I had packed the bags for us.

"Well, Mr. Manchester, you packed our bags?"

"Yes, I did, Mrs. Manchester. It was the helpful thing to do."

Alexis moved in to kiss me when my work phone rang. *That is just Carlton*, I thought. A part of me wanted to answer, but I was tired of being his bitch. After my honeymoon, I would have my boys raid his place. This was becoming a hassle.

Wesley

Alexis came through and spent the day with me. Before she had left, she hit me with some big news. Her ass was pregnant and was almost one hundred percent sure that it was mine. We planned to get a blood test as soon as she got back in town.

For sure, it was time for me to stop hitting the streets. I hated that she even married that whack-ass cop now. She should be here with me. I wondered if she told him that she was pregnant. I was pissed, not to mention his ass was still fucking with me and my crew.

Carlton had to be telling him where the drop off was. He raided left and right. Elle and Afon were pissed, and I had to come up with a solution. Therefore, tonight, I gave Carlton a different location than I did Elle. I told Afon that Carlton was trying to ruin me, and he simply said handle it. If I did, I could get myself clean. I wouldn't get out, but I would be sitting next to him.

Back to my snake-ass cousin. As soon as I gave his ass an address, I watched him make calls and send text messages. While at the bar, I had one of the strippers give him a drink laced with sleep aids. I had to have her get me his phone.

Let's pray that tonight's drink mixture wouldn't kill his snake ass. I just wanted to make sure that he was out cold, so I added four pills in some Crown, making sure the pills dissolved.

After his drink was served, Camille greeted me.

"Give me my fucking niece back," she demanded.

"What the fuck are you talking about?"

She ranted on about how we kidnapped her, and she showed me messages from Carlton. I fucking threw up in my mouth. Why the fuck would he do that?

"Look, Camille, I don't fuck with kids, not at all. I would've just shot ya ass in the stomach. Problem solved, no baby. Get the fuck out of my face and get Carlton."

She stared at me for a few moments and then walked away.

Carlton had to be stopped.

***

As soon as Alexis got back, she was at my apartment. I came home to her sitting on the counter. It was a lovely surprise. After us hugging and kissing, I wanted to jump all over her, but we needed to talk about our plan. First, I didn't want to risk her being seen coming in and out of my place. While she was gone, I rented a hotel an hour out of town. I told her that we could meet there weekly, squeezing in time around here. I had a plan to keep Chase on bogus ass runs. I called Carlton, telling him that I was at a run, giving him an address. There would be a small rival gang there, just to make it look as if the feds were cracking down on crime in general, and that would help to mend things with Elle.

I filled Alexis in on how Chase had been helping Carlton try to ruin me and how they were talking every day. I also told her that I thought that Carlton had done something to Camille's niece. I had been searching for her, but I couldn't find her. I still had time to find her, but it broke my heart. It had been a month, but I also hadn't heard from Camille since the day she told me. I had given Afon and Elle all the proof I had about Chase and Carlton working together. Man, he couldn't work that close with a cop in the world. He had better hope that he didn't end up dead first.

"Babe, we have to fake my death for us to get out. You need to be first on the scene, and I have the prefect victim."

"Okay, babe, that is a great idea."

We kissed, and soon, I was making love to her again. I texted Carlton five addresses that would keep Chase busy with paperwork while I made love to his wife.

CHAPTER TWELVE

Back to the Present
Carlton

My phone had been blowing up for hours. Finally, I noticed that it was Chase, and I wanted to know why the fuck he was calling me.

"What?" I yelled into the phone.

"Wesley is dead," Chase blurted out.

My soul jumped for joy after being pissed that I didn't get to kill his ass myself. Things all worked out. For a moment, I thought that he had figured out I was after him, but I was smarter.

"Again, why are you on my phone?"

"You are next of kin and will need to claim the body. He was set on fire, so it was a crime of passion. It will be on the news soon. We can't release a name yet. I just saw Alexis pull up."

"Tell her it is for the best. His ass needed to die."

"Carlton, now that Wesley is gone, our business is done."

"You are done when I say, and we aren't done. I need a partner."

He hung up on me and texted me an address. I got dressed and headed there. I hit up Afon and broke the bad news to him.

When I got there, some guy said that there was hair and an ID. That was how they knew that it was Wesley. My day had just gotten better, and Chase was about to take Wesley's spot, if he knew what was good for Alexis. Just as the thought left my head, Chase stood in front of me.

"Just the man I wanted to see," I said.

"What?"

"We need to take over the streets since Wesley is gone."

"We ain't doing shit."

"If you want to be with your wife, you will help me. The only person keeping her alive is YOU."

We glared at each other, and this was a crock of shit. He walked away, looking pissed. I would never let him forget that he was a cop. He helped me so far. Now, he was in too deep. Damn, I needed to get in touch with Camille. I returned her niece home; she was broken but would live to see another day. After I sent her home, I hadn't seen or heard from Camille. She quit dancing and went MIA.

Alexis

So far, our plan was going perfect. I had to chat with Chase. He had to break the news to me. I saw him talking with a few of his men until he saw me. He came over, placed his arms around my shoulders, and told me it was Wesley.

Now, it was time for me to give the performance of the year. I screamed and fell to the ground, crying like I had just lost my best friend. I wished I could've patted myself on the back a few times. Chase tried to comfort me, but he knew that I loved Wes all my life and that this would be hard for me.

I wouldn't see Wesley for a few days. Then, he would call me and let me know what to do next. I was worried he wouldn't want to go a few days without calling. I got a burner phone, so we should be cool. I just had to figure out how the hell I would get away from Chase. It had been two months since I found out that I was pregnant. Now, it was time to tell my husband but after I went live for breaking news.

After giving another Oscar-winning performance, I made my way back to work. I requested some time off, and my manager had a great idea. I should take a case that was out of town, so I could get a break. I declined because I needed the time off, but then again, it was a perfect cover story when I heard from Wesley. We had to make sure that our plan would work, and then, we would meet up. As soon as he called, I would be out of town with an assignment that would get me a few months off away.

***

It had been three weeks, and there was no word from Wesley. I guess he just used me to get away from all the madness, and he would leave me a single parent. I had to tell Chase that I was pregnant. I was starting to show.

I was walking away from my job to the car when I felt someone grab me from behind. I could feel a gun or what I thought was a gun in my back.

"Scream, Alexis, and I will blow your brains out."

That was the one and only Carlton. It was easier to just comply with his orders versus trying to see if he would really shoot me.

There was no need for small talk. He was talking to me for a reason; I just had no idea what he wanted. Since there was no Wesley, he really wouldn't leave me alone.

Then, it dawned on me. Whatever he wanted with me had to do with Chase. Damn, what type of mess did he get me into?

To my surprise, he only took me to the club. He told me that I needed to call Chase and tell him that I had six hours to live if he didn't comply. As soon as Chase answered the phone, I told him that I was pregnant, and I had been kidnapped because he was working with the enemy, and now, I would die.

Carlton didn't give us much time to chat. After I said my peace, he locked me in a room, saying that he would be back. He had to teach Chase a lesson. He just wanted to fuck me.

"You don't have to rape me. I will just have sex with you," I pleaded.

He didn't force himself on me, but he did have sex with me and recorded it. I cried the whole time as he had a gun next to my head. It had to be hours later, and I was lying in a bed, feeling like the dirtiest person in the world. Finally, the burner phone rang.

"Alexis, I got us a place."

Those were the best words I had heard, but how in the hell did I get out of here?

"Carlton has me. I can't meet you. I have no clue how to get out."

"Where are you?"

"At the club, in the bedroom."

"Behind the bookcase is a door. It leads you to the basement. Inside the wine cellar, go to the right, and there is a door. Find Chris and he will take you to the bus station. You leave with the shirt on your back and call this number. I will tell you where to go."

The line went dead, and I made my way to the cellar. All the way to the bus station, I called the number back, and there was no answer. I went on the first bus out. I guess Alexis was on her own.

Wesley

What the fuck was going on? I couldn't believe Carlton was behind this shit.

I walked outside, needing some air.

I know he's blood, but I'm definitely going to fuck him up once I have Alexis in the clear, I thought as I hit the blunt of exotic.

As much as she was a pain in the ass, Alexis was my rib, my last breath.

An hour later, I still hadn't heard from Alexis. She said that she was already in route, so what was the fucking hold up? I had called her several times, and the phone went straight to voicemail.

"Fuck, where she at?" I growled.

I put the blunt out and brushed some loose ashes off of my Ralph Lauren shirt. "Her ass is going to be the death of me," I said to myself as I put my chrome, pearl-handled 9mm in my shoulder holster.

Twenty minutes later, I pulled up to the bus terminal. I saw a few people standing outside, waiting on the bus. I walked inside the station. It was the size of a storefront. The station was weathered; the dingy white paint was peeling off of the walls. It had a row of plastic seats that were full of people waiting for their bus. The ticket processor was an older, white woman who looked like she tanned a lot because her skin looked like shiny leather.

"Next," she barked. I stepped forward toward the counter.

"Yes, I was wondering if the bus from Charlotte has arrived yet?" I smiled.

"Yes, it came and left about thirty minutes ago," she answered.

I brushed my hand over my face, visibly aggravated and concerned. Seeing my mannerisms change, she asked, "Is there anything else I can help you with, sir?"

Wondering where she was had my thoughts, but her announcing the next bus helped me refocus. "Thank you for everything." I smirked as I turned on my heel to leave.

"You're welcome," she responded as I exited.

Minutes later, I was sitting in my car. I pulled out my cell phone to call her, but I only got her voicemail.

"Fuck, I hope she ain't on no dumb shit," I yelled as my hand hit the steering wheel. I was past pissed. "She knows motherfuckers thinking I'm dead, so I want to keep it that way 'til the right time," I muttered to myself as I sped out of the parking lot.

After getting back to what I thought would be our new place, it dawned on me that I had told her to use a burner phone. As soon as the car was parked, I rushed in the house and found that phone, realizing that I had missed a call from Alexis.

Damn, I missed my baby's call. She must think that I am playing her.

"FUCK!" I yelled.

Calling Alexis back from the burner phone, there was no answer, so I called again. Finally, after the third call, she answered the phone.

"Hello."

"Where are you?"

"I don't know, but I was heading to Ohio."

"What the fuck is in Ohio? You need to turn around and come to Raleigh."

"You need to make sure you answer the phone because I am not going to be going on a wild goose chase."

"Please, Alexis, just turn around. I was calling your phone. I had totally forgot that you had to get rid of that phone."

"I actually think Raleigh is the next stop."

"I will be there waiting."

Yes, I was about to have my baby back in my arms.

142

CHAPTER THIRTEEN

Carlton

This dumb ass cracker knew I had him by his balls. He had Camille and an unborn baby's death on his hands. So, in my eyes, he was my bitch. With Wesley dead, the city belonged to me and the Gucci crew. I knew having Alexis as a pawn was my guarantee. I had to admit taking out Wesley was fucked up, but he made himself a liability when he let his little head take over.

"Money over bitches every day," I chimed.

Big Tony had just walked into my office.

"What's goodie, boss man?" joked Tony as he sat down on the couch.

"Nothing much, just playing mental chess." I smirked.

"Aye, yo. You know Wesley's murder is the talk on the streets and the news," he responded.

I dropped my head and gave a solemn look to his statement.

"Sorry for your loss. Whoever the motherfucker was that did it, I will bring you their head personally," Big Tony assured me.

"Wesley was like a brother to me."

I knew I had to change the subject, so I asked, "So, what all of our traps looking like?"

Tony gave me a look like he was picking up on how I changed the subject.

"We good on work," he answered. "Man, I bet it was behind that bougie bitch, Alexis, that got him killed," snarled Tony. "You mind if I smoke?" Tony asked me as he pulled out a blunt.

I waved him off and said, "When have you ever had to ask? Nicca, blaze that bitch up."

"You know a nicca need that for my nerves."

"Yo, Tony, I need you to get that young girl out of here."

"Dead or alive?"

"Alive then shoot the son of a bitch that was fucking her."

Tony nodded his head, showing that he agreed with what I had said.

The door flew open, and one of my men rushed in.

"Boss, Alexis is gone!"

"Gone, what the fuck? I need her, so somebody better find the bitch and do it fast," I commanded.

Who in the hell could have helped her escape?

145

Chase

"Bro, I am at the Mega station, and I see Alexis getting on a bus," Malone, one of my undercover workers, said.

Where the fuck is she going? I thought to myself before replying. "Thank you. She must be going to see a friend."

After hanging up the phone with him, I called Alexis, and there was no answer. I called a few friends and had an office at every bus station. She was smart. She had paid with cash, and I had no clue where she was going, but I was going to find out and make her ass explain where the fuck she was going. She would not leave me and live to talk about it.

An hour later, Malone called me, saying that he had her ass and would wait for my shift to end to meet up with me. My next destination was the crib. Since I had been working with Carlton, I had plenty money to spare. It was time that Alexis and I went on another field trip. This time, I was going to show her ass that I was the fucking boss. She was going to do what I said when I said it. It was time for her to be a wife and have this fucking baby.

Yes, I knew that the baby wasn't mine, but if she wanted to have that bastard child then I'd allow it. I mean,

Wesley's ass was dead, so I'd be the only dad that the kid knew.

Two weeks ago, I purchased Alexis and I a new house. That was where I was going to take her.

Camille

The sound of my cell phone buzzing caused me to damn near jump out of my bed. The clock showed two thirty a.m. *Who the fuck is calling me this late?* I thought as I picked up the phone. It was my sister, Sheena.

"Hello," I answered.

"My baby is gone," she screamed in my ear.

My heart fell to the floor as tears flooded my eyes. I always thought that Carlton was a piece of shit. Now, I knew two hundred percent that he was the worst person I had ever met in my life. I swore to God they were all going to pay for this.

"Where are you? What happened?" I asked.

"At the hospital. Someone sat her on the neighbor's porch. They thought that she was trying to rob them, and he shot her. By the time we made it the hospital, she was gone. Camille, my baby is gone. What the fuck am I going to do?"

"I am on my way."

The line went dead, and tears fell down my eyes. Carlton, Wesley, Chase, and Alexis would pay for this. I couldn't believe that Carlton would do this. If he hadn't kidnapped her, she would still be alive. My anger would not allow me to grieve.

I had no idea what the fuck I was going to do to them, but I swore on this baby's life it was going to be so fucking bad. The best thing about it was they were not going to see me coming.

Alexis

So much bullshit had happened the last couple of months that I didn't know if I was coming, going, or just went. At this point, it didn't even matter. I was excited to see Wesley. It had been a long three weeks.

I had to find a way to get rid of Carlton's ass. I couldn't believe that son of a bitch had sex with me. Tears formed in my eyes. I was tired of this shit. Why did I ever go back?

The bus stopped at a rest area. *Thank God*, I thought, damn near running to the get off the bus. My bladder was about to explode. Once off the bus, I rushed into the bathroom. Once I finished washing my hands, there was a sharp pain as I turned. His hand damn near spun me around.

***

I woke up in the back of Malone's funky ass car. It smelled like hell and death warmed over. After the aroma filled my nostrils, the urge to vomit hit me. Sitting up to throw up, the door would not open.

"FUCK!" I screamed.

What if Carlton had me again? What was he going to do with me now? My heart started to race, and out came more throw up, this time all over the backseat.

"You dumb bitch. You will squalor in your mess," fussed Malone.

"You're really a piece of shit," I scoffed.

The cigar he was smoking invaded the interior of the car. I sighed, seeing he was showing no compassion.

Wesley

It had been three hours and no Alexis. I drove back to the bus station and showed her picture to some of the people getting off the bus, and they said that she didn't get back on the bus at the rest stop. Something was definitely wrong with her. I had to figure it out. *Damn*, I thought, walking back to the car.

I was going to find Alexis. But right now, I had no idea how.

Fuck!

Carlton better not have her ass again. There was only one person that knew I was alive, and that was Chris. I only trusted him as far as I could kick him. But I hit him up anyway.

"Yo, C, where is Alexis? Does Carlton have her?"

"No, boss. He just realized that she was missing. Tell me what to do and I'm on it."

"Keep your ears to the ground, follow the cop, and let me know what's happening." I ended the call after that. See, Chris had been my eyes and ears for a while. He was just a young thug trying to get to the top.

Damn, I needed a plan. So far, he had been on point, telling me what was going on.

***

I was pissed, driving around, trying to figure out what the hell was going on. Alexis's ass should have been on the bus. I bet Carlton had a hand in her not making it on that bus as we planned. All this shit was weighing a nicca down, but for my cousin to try to take me out had me fucked up. I bet her ass went back to Chase's punk ass. *Fuck her*, I thought to myself as I headed back to my spot to figure out how I was going to dead Carlton's ass.

Fifteen minutes later, I was pulling into my garage. I had bought this house five years ago. It sat on the outskirts of Huntersville. It was a brick colonial house with four bedrooms and two and half baths. It sat at the bottom of a dirt road. No neighbors for miles. I closed the garage door and walked into the side entrance. In hindsight, I was glad I never told Carlton's snake ass about this place.

I went straight to the bar and poured me a shot of Crown Royal. After I poured my drink, I plopped down in my La-Z-Boy recliner. I know first I had to figure out why Carlton tried to take me out and then what the fuck was up with Alexis.

CHAPTER FOURTEEN

Chase

What the fuck is she doing at the bus station? I thought to myself as I sat in my office.

Carlton's bitch ass just called me earlier, trying to use her as leverage to blackmail me. I was going to let this shit play out and see what kind of shit he was on. Little did he know that he was on limited time. Seeing that Camille and Wesley were enjoying the afterlife, there were no more complications for me and Alexis's happy ever after. If she was still tripping, she would be bait food as well. I was getting excited that Malone happened to see her because I was trying to figure out what Carlton would want in return for her release. It was time to knock his ass down a notch or two. I couldn't put it all on him. I made a deal with the devil, and now, he was expecting to settle the books. I knew this sounded harsh, but whoever killed Wesley, I would give them a get out of jail free card. As I was getting enthralled in my excitement, I was interrupted by my phone ringing. I quickly answered, expecting it to be Malone. "Hello," I answered.

"So, what are you willing to give for your bitch?" snarled a confident Carlton.

I sighed before I answered. "Kill her. She's nothing but a pain in my ass." I could tell that my comment caught him off guard.

"W-W-What the fuck you say?" stuttered Carlton.

I boasted. "Kill the bitch because I'm not about to be blackmailed by you."

"Be mindful of your words," he snapped because he saw his intimidation tactic wasn't working.

"Get the fuck off my phone and do what you gonna do," I laughed. I ended the call, waiting on Malone's call. I couldn't believe Carlton's clown ass tried to play me like that.

Carlton

I knew something was up because Chase's ass was too cocky. I looked over at Big Tony, then I said, "How long had you been in here before you came to holler at me?" I questioned Tony.

He frowned at my question. "You doubting my loyalty? What you trying to say?" he chimed. I shot him a stone-faced expression because I was dead ass serious.

"Did I stutter, motherfucker?" I reiterated as I sat my 9mm on my desk.

Tony saw that I was serious. He didn't buck at my change in demeanor. I could tell he was insulted by my comments because he didn't answer. He simply dropped his head, then he said, "Nigga, I have killed for you, I have done bids for you, and you dare question my loyalty?"

Maybe I was tripping. My whole plan was going south real quick. Tony raised up from where he was sitting then said, "If you think I'm a foul ass nicca, squeeze the motherfucking trigger now."

Knowing I was wrong, I rose up as well, diffusing the tension by extending my hand and saying, "You right, dawg. I'm tripping."

Neither of us were scared. We both were killers who weren't much for bullshit. Tony left me hanging. As he dropped, he said, "I'm out. I see you're on some bullshit."

I would be pissed as well, so I respected his reaction. Moments later, I heard the door closing behind him. I shook my head because I had to find Alexis's ass. She was the leverage I needed to guarantee safe delivery for our dope shipments. I didn't need his happy ass doing any surprise raids on any of our trap houses. I didn't need any added stress from the Russians. I still had an ace in the hole. I had a few blue coats on the payroll. I hadn't heard anything about Camille's murder. I pulled out my phone and dialed an old friend's number, who had been down with us since day one.

"This is Malone. Who is this?" he gruffed.

"This is an old friend," I answered.

He paused mid statement then joked, "All my old friends are dead."

I knew his racist ass would be on some dumb shit. "I know a man who needs someone found," I chimed.

He got quiet, then he responded, "Is this you, Cornbread?"

"Yes, this is me, you old, Irish, racist fuck," I shot back.

"Who is the missing person?" he inquired.

"Alexis Manchester," I responded.

"Hmmm, hmmm," was his response. "How much are you paying? By the way, my condolences about Wesley," he quipped. "Well, Cornbread, you're in luck. I have her in my possession right now."

"Stop shitting me," I barked, slightly aggravated at how this situation was unraveling.

"Thank you for your condolences. He was like a brother to me," I lied.

"You think she killed Wesley?" he questioned.

"No, I just need to see if she knows anything," I lied again.

"How much is this job paying? I could give a fuck what you want with her," he boasted.

"I told you all my friends dead. Franklin, Lincoln, all them old fucks are my concern."

"So, seriously, you have her in your possession?" I questioned with skepticism.

"Didn't I tell you I have her? I caught her at the bus station. Your buddy, Chase, is waiting on her as well," he said, thinking his greedy ass would get more money.

"Two hundred thousand. Take it or leave it," I growled, knowing he would bite.

"Hmmm, okay, where can we meet?" he quickly questioned.

"Put her on the phone," I demanded.

The phone went silent. I heard some ruffling, and then, minutes later, I heard him say,

"Speak into the phone, bitch."

I heard a faint woman's voice say, "You will regret this."

Then more background noise then a female voice finally said, "Hello. Who is this?"

I was convinced it was Alexis. My only response was, "Put Malone back on the phone."

"I don't have all day. Where are we meeting?" Malone snapped, sounding slightly aggravated, waiting on me to respond.

"Let's meet over by Old Concord Road," I answered as I ended the call.

Alexis

"You know Chase gonna kill your old ugly ass," I spat.

My face was burning, and I knew I had a bruise from him punching me. Malone laughed at my comments.

"Shut the fuck up," Malone snapped at me.

His car smelled of sweaty ass cigars. From what I had seen of Malone, he looked like a heavy drinker. He was unshaven, and his clothes were wrinkled and worn. He was overweight with very unkempt grey hair. I was laying long ways in the backseat, hog tied.

"So, you really want to throw your career away?" I questioned him. I could tell by his sighs and grunts that he was getting aggravated.

As I was about to say something else, he slammed the car in park. I rolled and slammed into the backseat, face first. "What the fuck?" I yelped as I was now face up on the floor of the backseat.

As I was writhing in pain, Malone snapped the back door open.

"I'm tired of your mouth, bitch," he chimed.

Not giving a shit if I was injured or not, he pulled out a roll of grey tape, taping my mouth.

"Talk now, bitch," he joked.

Shit had got real, and tears rolled down my eyes. I was truly hating Wesley's ass right about now.

"I don't hear you saying shit now, fucking cunt."

Malone was staring at me like I was Sunday dinner with the fixings. I was now truly frightened. "You must have some good pussy," Malone teased. "Wesley's dead behind your ass. Chase is just plum stupid, wanting you back after you was fucking that nigga. Did Carlton fuck you too because he's paying two hundred thousand for your ass," snarled Malone.

Battered and bruised, I wasn't going to let this piece of shit, dirty cop break me. I sucked up my tears. I heard his phone going off. As crazy as it sounded, I was wishing it was Chase.

"Malone," he answered.

"Where are you?"

"She got away. That's one feisty jigaboo you got," his redneck ass lied. "I went to put her in the car, and she kneed me in the nuts. I been looking for her all day, chief."

I'm on it," was the last words he spoke as their call ended.

I reported on corruption. Now, I was experiencing it firsthand. I was repulsed at how easily this motherfucker lied.

This motherfucker was Chase's best man in our wedding. They said money was the root of all evil. I said it was what the evil people would do to get ahead.

Wesley

I was woken up by Chris's call.

"Wassup, dawg?" I answered.

Chris sounded frantic. "Bruh, your cousin on some grimy shit. Big Tony told me Carlton was bitching about Alexis escaping. And he said something about killing some cops as well."

"You didn't tell him I'm still alive, right?" I asked.

"No, boss. I kept that information to myself," Chris confirmed.

Still half asleep, I fired up the half smoked blunt in the ashtray.

"Oh, also I saw Camille's niece. I heard she got wet up," he said.

I was instantly zoning from the exotic, but I was all in when he mentioned Camille's people.

"What the fuck happened?" I questioned.

"Somebody wet her little ass up and left her on the porch." He repeated. "Shit been lit since you dipped."

I wanted to ask about Camille's snake ass, but I really didn't give a fuck. Dumb ass bitch trying to put a seed on me.

164

"I will hit you back when I have some real shit," said Chris.

"I need you to stay on Chase's ass also," I ordered.

"I got you, boss," responded Chris.

"Is there any word on Alexis?"

"Not yet but I have a crew outside working on it. They are posted at her house, and I had someone put a tracker on the white boy's car."

"Just keep me in the loop," I said before we disconnected the call.

Carlton

"Yo, I'm on my way with the bitch. It's gonna cost you triple because I had to lie to my best friend."

"Just get me the bitch asap."

"Naw, boy, you need to put the money in my account before I do anything."

I laughed. This piece of shit thought that he was going to run me. He had me so fucked up. I swore as soon as he got here, I was putting two in his head. Good help was so hard to find, I swear.

"Like I said, bring me the bitch and then I pay you."

"FUCK YOU."

He screamed in the phone before the line went dead.

Damn it!

I sent out a text, telling all my men to meet me at the spot.

One hour later, my whole crew was sitting in front of me.

"So, I got some information today. I heard the white cop, Chase, and his buddy, Malone, had Wesley killed. We need to watch their every move then kill them like the snakes that they are."

"We can't just kill cops, boss," one of the men yelled.

Pulling my Glock out its holster, pointing the gun at him, I squeezed the trigger.

"Does anyone else have problems with my plans?" I questioned.

Everyone shook their heads no.

"Somebody clean this mess up."

CHAPTER FIFTEEN

Chase

The worst feeling in the world was having to question your friend's loyalty. I met Malone back in grade school. We instantly clicked, so he would not betray me, right? Even if he did, what would drive him to stab me in the back? Shit, something wasn't right with his story about Alexis getting away. It was a good thing there were trackers on all of our phones. I GPS'ed his location. He should have known that I would track him. Once his location was discovered, I'd phone the local authorities and have him located. If he was lying to me, then he would meet his maker.

The desk phone rang, and there was a homicide that involved a teenager. The family was at the emergency department waiting for us to arrive. *There's work to be done*, I thought while leaving my office.

Twenty-five minutes later, I was at the hospital, shocked to see a very pregnant Camille. Every part of me wanted to shoot that bitch in the stomach. Another part of me wanted the bitch to suck me off. When she saw me, she walked away. I texted a fellow officer and told him to arrest her ass as soon as she left here.

Thirty minutes later, the report was complete. Malone had been spotted. From the intel I received, he was by himself. I couldn't have him pulled without probable cause. I couldn't bring my off–duty officers' participation in illegal activities to light. I would deal with Malone in due time. Alexis always told me he was a snake.

The hospital emergency room was crowded and loud. Camille saw me from a distance and mouthed that I wasn't shit as she extended her middle finger. I grimaced at her gesture. The fact that I wanted to fuck her up was written all over my face. She pouted her lips. The bitch thought she was safe.

"Motherfucker, I wish you would," someone yelled over my shoulder.

I quickly turned to see what the hell was going on.

"You son of a bitch better get your hands off of me," fussed an older man as he was resisting arrest.

I walked over to the officers to see what had happened. There was a woman with two black eyes and a swollen nose. He kind of reminded me of the guy who played Debo in that movie, *Friday*.

"Excuse me, ma'am, you need to step back," I said to who I assumed was the man's wife.

"Elroy, calm the hell down," she spat, holding her chest.

"Ma'am, please back up," I asked her as I stepped in front of her.

Just as I did, I felt a blow to the back of my head as I fell forward.

"Motherfucker, don't touch her," were the last words I heard before it went dark. I smacked the floor face first. Minutes later, I awakened, surrounded by uniformed officers.

"Chief are you okay?" one of my officers said as I blinked my eyes, trying to regain my composure.

My head was throbbing as the EMTs made their way through the crowd. Twenty minutes later, they had checked me out. I sat on the side of a gurney as onlookers, medical staff, and cops were crowded around. My face was numb, and by the look on some of their faces, I knew I had taken a bad spill.

"Chief, I'm advising you to let me check you out thoroughly," advised the E.R. doctor.

Usually, I would follow the doctor's order, but I had some unfinished business to attend to. I quickly looked around the room, noticing that Camille had slipped out. Fuck, her ass got away. The doctor stepped closer to me, flashing a little light on my face.

"Doc, I'm fine. I'm strong like a Tonka truck." I laughed.

"Chief, you need to be checked for a concussion, but I see you're ignoring me. I wish you the best." He walked off.

I gave my arresting officers the nod to make a detour. They were to fuck the belligerent man up who had hit me.

"Please don't take him," pleaded his wife, who was sitting behind me, sobbing.

"He assaulted an officer, ma'am," I explained to her to no avail.

I was really hating all niggers after all I had been through. Lately, it seemed like every set of eyes were looking at me. I quickly walked through the automatic exit doors. Soon as I was outside, I dialed the dispatcher to get me a location on Malone. I made it to my car and hurriedly opened the door, so I could see the damage the fall did to my face.

"Fucking niggers," I blurted out, examining my bruised face.

The way I was feeling, Carlton didn't want to fuck with me anymore today. I dialed arresting officer Emerson's number.

"Did you take that nigger on a detour before booking him?"

Usually, I was color blind, but lately, niggas didn't know their places. Like Alexis's ass, the nigger part of her biracial ass had her acting stupid.

"Good job, Emerson. I will remember this. I owe you one," I responded.

"No problem, boss," he said as I ended the call.

I crunk my car, still waiting on the GPS info for Malone. My first stop would be Carlton's club. I was in an asshole mood, plus I needed to show him who was the boss. I wanted him to talk shit, so I could have more reason to raid all of the trap houses.

Camille

Chase was the last person that I expected to see at the fucking hospital. I was hoping to lay low a little longer, but that would not be the case. My plan was still going to be put in effect. I just had to make it a little faster. I was sure that Chase would be calling Carlton and telling his bitch ass that I was still pregnant. *Damn*, I said to myself as I got in my car. I was blessed to have a man who thought that I was pregnant for him.

My sweet Sam decided that I needed to stop being a dancer and got me a nice condo along with a new car. I got to sit at home, eat, and get fat. Chase wouldn't be able to track me down cause the shit wasn't even in my name. One thing that they failed to realize about me was that I would make it no matter what. My momma raised me to be a survivor. I could hear her now. "Honey, you better sell that pussy if you have to. Hell, I sold mine to take care of y'all." That memory made me chuckle and cry all at the same time. I missed my momma. Lord bless her sweet soul.

The sound of Rihanna's *Sex With Me* brought my attention back to the present. Reaching in my purse to grab my phone, I knew it was Sam. He should just be getting to my place. Once the phone was in my hand, I swiped it.

173

"Hello."

"Baby, where are you?"

"On my way home, babe. Sorry I didn't cook dinner. I received some horrible information, and I didn't have time to cook."

"It's okay, luv. I have a surprise for you anyway."

Thirty minutes later, I was stepping in the house, and I could smell cookies and something else. It smelled divine. Sam spoiled me. He was a good man to me and his wife. Yes, he was married, but hell, bitches had to learn how to share the dick if they wanted to keep it cause a bitch like me came for it all.

After dinner, we took a bubble bath together. Once out, Sam gave me a full body massage. The next thing I wanted to do was fuck the shit out of him, but he had to go. The weekend would be here soon enough, and I would have him all to myself.

Once my bae was gone, I downloaded a free text app. It was time to put my plan into action. First, I was going to hit Carlton and Chase where it hurt the most... in their fucking pockets. Let the games begin, bitches.

Alexis

It had been hours, and Malone was just driving around. The smell of his cigars had me sick as a fucking dog. At the rate I was going, I would die from choking on my throw up. Tears were running down my eyes like streams. I was fucked up right now. I fought the urge to throw up in a desperate attempt to save my fucking life. Hell, I was wondering if he was using me to trap Chase.

Finally, the car stopped, and I heard the car door open. Then, terror hit me when I heard Carlton's voice.

"Malone, where is the bitch.?" I heard Carlton yell.

"I told you I want double the money, boy."

"I told you that I wasn't giving you double."

Then, I heard someone say, "Kill this cracker." Three shots later, the car was moving again. My heart was racing. *Damn, what the fuck is about to happen now?* I thought.

"Bitch, you know your time is limited," sneered Carlton after he killed Malone.

If my mouth wasn't taped, I would have called Carlton a two pump nigga with his little ass dick. He would never be half the man that Wesley was. Hell, Chase had a bigger dick. No wonder I had more fun fucking myself than I did fucking him.

The last thing I heard from Carlton was him yelling, "Take that bitch back to the spot. I have a few runs to make."

Now, I was stuck in the car with his goons, Big Tony and Chris. At least these clowns were less abrasive than Malone. The one guy, Chris, kept peeking at me through his visor mirror. I found it odd that when he was handling me, he untied me instead of keeping me bound. Chris and Big Tony were actually too decent to be two of my captors.

"Ayeooooo, I need to take a piss," he blurted out.

Tony was about to respond when his phone rang.

"Wassup, boss?" he answered. "Where we at?"

Chris looked around then answered. "We just passed Jackson Training School."

Chris finally pushed his visor up.

"Okay, boss. We're on our way," confirmed Tony.

Chris tapped Tony on his leg.

"Stop by this gas station so I can piss. Please, like I really need to go, and I bet she has to go as well. She's pregnant, and you know pregnant chicks always gotta pee."

Tony grimaced at Chris's request as he pulled off onto a deserted road. As soon as he parked the car, they both jumped out. Tony evidently went to take a shit. He was scurrying for paper but ended up grabbing the newspaper. I sat in the car with my mouth taped and hands tied in the front. I knew it sounded crazy, but I believed that my chances of survival were better with these guys. It was warm out, and the breeze coming through the front window cooled me down. I was a little parched. Hopefully, these guys would have enough common sense to check on me. Where we were parked was isolated. The heat had me miserable. Sweat was stinging my eyes. I saw Chris appear from the bushes. He was making his way to the car.

As he got closer, I heard Tony yelp. "Hey, man, bring me some more newspaper."

"Okay, I got you," Chris yelled back.

Chris looked at me as he opened the passenger side door. I saw him grab a gun off the seat that he wrapped in the newspaper. I gasped. This day was like watching a mob movie in 3D.

"Do you still need the newspaper?" Chris asked Tony, but I knew something was about to go down. Minutes later, I saw Tony's hand.

"What the fuck, dog?" I heard Tony whine as he was now in my view with newspaper in hand, his pants around his ankles.

"It's nothing personal, dog," growled Chris as he threw Tony a phone. He backed away. He ran to the car, gently pulling the tape off my mouth.

"I am going to get you somewhere safe," he said in a soft, assuring tone.

Minutes later, Chris was backing the car out. Whew, I was glad he didn't kill Tony. He seemed like a cool guy the few minutes I was around him. Chris sped off, leaving Tony behind.

"Can I please have some water please?" I begged.

Chris drove a little while longer then pulled onto a side road. He walked around to my side of the car with a bottle of water in his hand. He put his gun in the small of his back as he opened the door.

"Lean forward," he ordered.

I scooted forward as he freed my hands. My throat was drier than the desert as I grabbed the bottle of Dasani water from him. I turned the bottle up, drinking all the water in less than thirty seconds.

"Are you hungry?" he asked.

It dawned on me that he was the one who had helped me escape the first time. The only one that Wes could trust.

"A little but I can wait until we get to a safe place," I replied.

"First, we have to get rid of this cop car."

We drove about thirty minutes, and there was a parked car in the middle of the woods. He jumped out the car then helped me out. He poured gas around the car, lit a cigarette, took a few puffs, then threw it to the car. Quickly, we got into the other car and sped off.

***

I woke up to the car stopping at a big yellow house. I had no idea where the hell I was. Honesty, it was good that he did not take me to Carlton. I had lived to see another day, but I was scared as hell. Once in the house, Chris made a call. He whispered a few things then brought me the phone. It was Wesley. The sound of his voice made me relax. He said that he would see me in three days. What the hell! Three days! That was way too long! I figured that Wes had no idea where the fuck he was going. Before Wes told me that he loved me, he said that Chris would guard me with his life, and it only made me feel a lot better. All I wanted to do was eat and go to sleep.

Chris left and went to get me some chicken and some clothes. While he was away, I sat in the hot bath, trying to make sense of what the fuck had just happened. This shit only happened in movies. I had technically been kidnapped three times in twenty-four hours, like what the fuck. Wesley needed to hurry up because I needed to be in his arms.

Chase

It took three fucking hours to get to Malone. Imagine my shock when we found his ass dead. Man, how the fuck did someone beat me to the punch? His car had not been located, so I still didn't know where the fuck my baby was. "Damn," I yelled into the air, and a few of my officers looked at me. We needed to find his car. There weren't too many cops that I could trust, so I did not want to blurt out, "Find Alexis."

The CSI team arrived, and I got in my car. Carlton better not have my wife, or there was going to be hell to pay. I called Tommy and told him that we needed to raid all the houses that Carlton and Wesley had owned. I was finding Alexis tonight if it was the last thing that I do.

My phone rang, and the number was unknown. "Manchester," I answered.

"It is good to talk you, Chase. I hope you like the gift that I left for you."

"Carlton, you leave Alexis out of this," I commanded.

Carlton burst into laughter before saying, "Just a few hours ago, you were saying kill the bitch. Not so tough now. Huh, Chase?"

"You will pay for this. I swear I will cut your nuts off and feed them to you."

"Chase, the ball is now in my court. You are my bitch, and you will do what the fuck I say when I say. Don't forget that I fixed your problem."

"I saw my problem today, and the bitch is still pregnant. I don't owe you shit."

"You saying that Camille is still pregnant?"

"Yes, I seen the bitch. Her niece was killed, and there she was at the hospital. Funeral arrangements are being made."

"I will take care of that bitch, but I will not give you Alexis back until you make these moves with me. You knew that once Wesley was gone you were in."

"Fuck you, Carlton. This is war! You have fucked with the wrong white boy."

"No, Chase, you fucked with the wrong nigga. You will see."

The line went dead. We had just declared war.

Wesley

I was sitting outside, enjoying the weather, when I got a call from Chris. He told me that he had Alexis, and he was taking her to a safe house in Atlanta, GA which was good. I needed to shower first then I would hit the road. I was smiling all the way to the bathroom, taking the quickest shower. While I was in the shower, Chris texted me the address to where they would be staying. I texted him back, asking him to not tell Alexis that I was on the way.

Once I was on the road, five hours later, I was at the safe house where my baby was. I missed her smart-ass mouth having self so much.

I knocked on the door, and Chris opened it.

"Where is my baby?"

"She went to lay down. She said that she had a headache. She is in the first room on the right."

Rushing down the hall, I saw two open doors and one closed. I tried to open it, but it was locked. I beat on the door like I was the police, and she opened it, looking sexy as fuck, showing off her stomach. Her breasts were full and round. She was wearing only a t-shirt and maybe some panties.

We stared at each other, then she jumped in my arms. We kissed and hugged. She smelled like flowers. After a few more hugs, I picked Alexis up and walked into the room. She pushed the door closed while we walked to the bed. Gently, I laid her down on the bed then straddled her. We kissed again while I debated if I was going to fuck her slow or beat her pussy out the frame.

Alexis looked up at me, saying, "What the fuck are you waiting for, Wesley? I need you to fuck me."

"I'm going to, but we need to make a plan."

She rolled her eyes at me before saying, "Do we not have all night and all day tomorrow to talk? Can't we just enjoy each other's company for a moment please?"

She looked as if she was about to cry. I could see that pregnant Alexis was going to drive a nigga crazy.

I stared at her for a few moments then slowly but passionately kissed her, pulling her t-shirt up. Alexis let out a moan as I broke the kiss to explore her body. At first, we were making eye contact, then she closed her eyes while I placed one breast in my mouth and massaged the other one. All of a sudden, she began crying, like really bawling.

"What's wrong, baby?"

No words left her mouth, just sobs. What the fuck did I just do? Did I hurt her? "Alexis, honey, talk to me please. What's wrong?"

All she managed to say was Carlton.

"Alexis, suck that shit up and tell me what the fuck is wrong with you." She stared at me blankly. Alexis appeared to be shocked by my attitude, but I needed to know what the fuck was wrong with her.

Just as fast as she started crying, she stopped and started to kiss me.

What the fuck just happened? I thought as I tried to get back in the mood.

Carlton

That white muthafucka thought that he could just talk to me any type of way, and he expected me to accept it. He had me fucked up. But I could show his ass better than I could tell him, and him seeing a pregnant Camille pissed me off. I spared her niece because she sent me abortion papers. That bitch was going to pay for lying to me. She then fucked up my deal with Chase. Fucking up my deal messed with my money, and when you fucked with my money, you had to die. *But who killed her niece?* I thought. That was not my problem. I should have killed the little bitch since Camille wanted to lie and pretend, but I had eyes and ears everywhere. I sent out a few text messages, telling my crew that I wanted eyes on her sister. I needed to know when they were having the funeral. I was going to pay for it. Get in good with the family.

I sat back and kicked my feet up on my desk, thinking about how I was going to fuck the shit out of Alexis while she was my prisoner, take more videos, send them to the cop, and make him my bitch. After I gained the control that I desired, I would go for the kill and take over the streets. A perfect plan. While I was in a daze, my door flew open. In waltzed Elle and Afon.

185

"Hello, what a pleasant surprise," I said, lying.

"We need to discuss what is going to happen since Wesley is no longer alive," Elle stated, plopping her skinny ass down in one of the chairs.

"What do you mean what is going to happen? I will run things," I replied, trying not to show my attitude.

"Word on the street is that you are working with the pigs." Afon added to the conversation, still standing and making me nervous as hell.

"I did blackmail a cop and make him run a route for me, but it was Chase. He is the husband to the bitch that Wes was fucking, and he was bringing heat on us, so I did what I had to do."

"Carlton, that was stupid to blackmail a cop. He could get you for extortion or later raid us. Wesley is gone, so what is keeping us safe?" Elle screamed.

"Bitch, lower your voice in my fucking office. I told you I have proof that I paid him and a few of his buddies. They aren't going to fuck with us," I shot back.

The Elle chick started to say some shit in a different language, and Afon looked very concerned. However, he did not say one thing. He just stared at me, and for a moment, I was feeling scared.

"What is your plan?" Afon finally asked, breaking our weird silence.

"I have kidnapped his bitch and set him up for murder. He will continue to comply, or his bitch will be dead."

As the words left my mouth, there was a knock at my door.

"I'm busy. Come back later," I yelled.

"They never arrived back in town, boss. What would you like us to do?"

"I want you to find them. NOW!"

Afon and Elle were glaring at me as I attempted to gain my composure. Why was it so hard to keep this bitch contained? That meant that I had an enemy in my camp, and he must be dealt with, but who the hell was the snake? Quickly pulling my attention back to them, I said,

"Everything is okay. You two have nothing to worry about."

"Things here seem out of control. We will need to have a meeting as soon as possible," Afon said.

"Okay, I will get with you soon about that," I lied. For once, we were going to do things my way.

Afon grabbed Elle by the hand, helping her get up. When she first sat down, her curvy body was not obvious, but now that she stood up and her fire red dressed hugged her small frame, damn the white bitch was kind of cute. Either way, the door opened, and those two were gone. I had to say I was happy as hell to see them go.

I made a mental note to see how the hell I could get Afon out the way.

Alexis

I wanted to make love to Wesley so bad, but the thoughts of Carlton having sex with me was invading my thoughts, giving me the urge to throw up. All I could do was cry. I knew that I freaked Wesley out because he was yelling at me. I wanted to tell him, but I had no idea how he was going to take this. All of this was going through my head, and now, I was unable to get wet. We were kissing, and I was not turned on at all. Finally, breaking the kiss, I decided that I needed to tell him.

"Wesley, Carlton forced me to have sex with him," I said.

"HE DID WHAT?"

"I am so sorry."

"Why the fuck are you sorry? This is not your fault, babe. I am sorry that you had to endure that, but I promise you Carlton will pay."

"I am sorry that I can't focus on having sex with you, and I want you so badly, but at the same time, I feel super dirty."

Wesley did not say anything else. He pulled me closer to him, kissing the top of my head. I fought back my tears. This was the first time anyone had ever held me while I sobbed. As Wesley held me, I felt something wet hit my head. Could it be that Wes was so mad that tears formed in his eyes? Wow, we were connecting like we had never connected before.

Looking up at him, it was my turn to hold him and assure him that this was not his fault. I sat up and pulled him to my exposed breast, putting his head right in the middle. Though we were sharing a moment, there was a part of me that was turned on. Forgetting all about Carlton, I pushed my breast to his face. He latched on like a newborn baby, and finally, my river began to flow as he sucked on my breast, and I rubbed my pussy. I moaned as he sucked harder and harder. My breasts being tender was a symptom of being pregnant, but today, pleasure was pain, and I took it. Rubbing faster and faster, my temperature started to rise, and my pussy started to pulsate. My breath became shallow and fast. Just as I was about to cum, I was flipped over, and Wes started to lick my pussy from behind. After licking the clit a few times, he started to suck on it, and I began to wiggle. It felt so good, and I was holding back. The last thing I wanted was the young boy hearing us, but he sucked harder, sliding his finger inside of me. My body was no longer my own. Wesley had me in some type of death grip as he sucked my soul away. I did not think that I had ever screamed so loud or been so wet in my life.

After cumming about three more times, and begging Wesley to stop, he entered me, letting out a loud moan as he fed me every inch of him.

"Did you miss this dick?" Wesley asked breathlessly.

I did not say anything at all. Who in the hell had time to talk when you were just trying to breathe? Wesley pushed the top of my back down. If it was at all possible, he was going in deeper. I let out a small scream.

Wesley sped up his movements and thrusted harder. I threw my ass back, finally getting into the groove, taking all that he was throwing at me.

Between breaths, I was finally able to ask, "Did you miss this pussy?"

Wesley grabbed me by the hair, making my head snap back. I let out a scream, but it was not from pleasure.

"Hey," I screamed.

"Did you miss this dick?" he asked again, just a little louder.

At that moment, I was about to cum, and all the words that I was about to say vanished.

All I could get out was, "Ooooo," and take deep breaths.

"Whose pussy is this?" he asked.

"It's… it's… OMG, MY GOD, I'M CUMMING."

Wesley somehow flipped me over in one quick movement. Next thing I knew, my legs were spread eagle. He was pounding, and I was cumming again. I was trying to catch my breath before I tried to work my hips.

"I wanna get on top," I called out.

Wesley completely ignored my request. He kept going and going, then he stopped, finally letting me get on top of him. Once I straddled him and starting slowly bouncing on his dick, I attempted to kiss him, and he moved his head.

That completely killed my mood, giving me an instant attitude.

"What the fuck is wrong with you, Wes?"

He pushed me to the side and got out the bed without saying a word. He grabbed his pants and left the room. *What the fuck just happened?* I thought as I slid back into my t-shirt. I didn't have any clothes, but the shower was calling my name.

I walked to the top of the step, hearing Wesley say, "I'm going back to kill my cousin."

That brought tears to my eyes. The last thing that I wanted to do was get Wesley back in. We were finally home free.

Now, the mission was to save Wesley.

CHAPTER SIXTEEN

Chase

My heart was racing. All I wanted to know was where in the fuck my wife was. This fucking nigger had taken her, and he was going to kill her. I cursed the day I ever met Wesley. He had ruined my fucking life. I wished I was the one who killed his ass. I would not have stabbed him, I would have put a bullet in his fucking head, blowing that nigger's brains out.

I was pissed to find Malone dead. I knew deep in my heart that he was going to sell me out, but I wanted to be the one to put his ass down. Now, I was going to see how I could make sure Carlton took the fall for him and Wesley.

I had a snitch that owed me one, and I had someone pick him up. He was waiting for me in my office. I walked into my office, and there he sat, looking nervous.

"Hello, Mike. I need you to put word out on the street for me. You need to say that Carlton had Wesley killed."

"Why would I do that? So, he can kill me?"

"Do you think I give a fuck if he kills you? This is what you do... Tell someone that you know will spread the word. That way it is not coming from you."

"I will do what I can, but I am not going to make any promises to you. I am not gonna put my life on the line for some cracker ass cop."

I slowly walked towards him, trying to look as calm as possible, but when we were face to face, I said, "You will do it my way, or you will not live to smoke your next round of crack. Now, get the fuck out my office before I kill your bitch ass."

He pushed his chair back and hauled ass out of my office. I needed to create a distraction as I still looked for Alexis. Everyone would be focused on their beef. Plus, I knew that Carlton had eyes in my department, so whether Mike snitched or not, he was dead. I did not give a fuck. One less crackhead on the streets. After he left, I knew it was time to pay Afon a visit. Twenty minutes later, I pulled in front of the Club Cabana. It was surrounded by Russian goons.

Do you really think Afon is going to talk to you? I thought to myself.

A few minutes later, I was entering the deserted club where eight guys were strategically positioned.

One of them asked, "What can I help you with? Krispy Kreme is on the other side of Charlotte."

The other guys burst out in laughter.

I felt disrespected and replied, "I am sure if I ask everyone in here for gun permits and green cards, I would have a squad car full of Russians." Silence replaced their laughter.

"Laugh now, motherfuckers," I fired back.

Our laughter was now replaced with silence.

"Okay, let's try this again, fellas," I responded. "I need to talk to Afon. Can y'all fine citizens help me?" I joked as I walked up.

The room was still silent when a door opened, and an older, Russian gentleman stepped out dressed in a blue tailored suit with Ferragamo loafers and asked, "How may I help you?"

"We are looking for Afon," I responded as he sat down.

"That would be me. How can I help you, officer?" he responded with a thick accent.

"Well, Mr. Afon, we're working on a murder case that happened a few days back," I lied. "We're thinking the victim maybe was an associate of yours, and I was wondering if you could answer a few questions for us," I chimed.

Afon's face grew dark as he grimaced. "So, does this supposed associate of mine have a name?"

"Yes, Wesley. He was a local plug known for flooding the local neighborhoods."

Afon looked like he was in deep thought and answered, "No, that name does not sound familiar." I looked at him, knowing he was lying and responded, "Well, thank you for your time, and if you hear anything, will you give me a call?" I said as I passed Afon my card.

"I am just a local business owner. I do not dabble in those circles, so I do not see where I can be of any assistance." responded Afon as he gave the card back.

"Well, our business is done here," I interjected, aggravated by Afon's responses.

Minutes later, I was driving toward Sugar Creek when I said out loud to myself, "I know that motherfucker's lying! Did you see how his whole demeanor changed when I mentioned Wesley's name?"

I pulled the dog's chain. Let's see if he barks or bites, I thought to myself.

"Let's just sit back, and let's see who makes the next move," I said aloud to myself as I wondered if Alexis was okay since she escaped from Malone. I had a hunch that Carlton had a hand in it.

Carlton

It had been some hours since I heard from Big Tony. I called his phone a few times, and there was no answer. What the fuck was going on? I wanted this bitch here so that I could make Chase's ass pay for all the shit that he had been talking. This cat had me fucked up. *Damn*, I thought while sitting at my desk.

Tony would be here by now, so something must be wrong. *We need to find them*, I thought as I gathered up a few members of my crew, and we hit the streets. Four hours later, there was still no sign of Tony. I had to call one of the cops that I had on my payroll. The phone rang three times before he answered.

"Nixon here."

"I need you to get a location of this number, 161-222-1222, or the last location. I can't find one of my men."

"Okay, I will call you back with details."

We disconnected the call. Stopping to get gas, I thought to myself that he better not be dead. Did Alexis get away, or did she have help? I could not imagine that Chris would betray me. I didn't know what the fuck was going on, but I swore I was going to get to the bottom of this shit. The sound of Jeezy's *Fuck You Pay* blasted as the phone vibrated in my hands. I quickly answered it because it was Nixon giving me the location of Tony along with saying that some crackhead named Mike was with Chase. There was a Judas in my camp, and that muthafucka had to be dealt with.

Once I had a location, it only took me a little over an hour to find Tony, and all he said was that Chris took Alexis and left. Maybe he was trying to save her out of loyalty to Wesley. As long as he returned her ass, I would not kill him. I was not saying that he wouldn't have consequences for his actions, but he would live to see another day... unless he was working for Chase.

Lately shit didn't seem to be going my way. Hell, the only good thing to happen was Wesley getting killed. When we were back to the spot, I called an emergency meeting. Once all my people were there, I announced that Big Tony was my new partner. He was Wesley's replacement. Some were amped about my decision, and I got a lot of bad looks. I also told them that we needed to find this Mike person, Chris, Camille, and Alexis. It needed to happen yesterday. They hauled ass out my spot.

"Damn, C, what the fuck are you gonna do next?" asked Tony as everyone dispersed after my announcement.

"I know we have to find Chris, see what he did with Alexis," I responded.

Tony gave me a bewildered look at my response.

"Well, everyone has their orders. I'm out of here," he said as he took his shot of Bourbon to the head.

"Aight, I need you on top of this, dawg," I spat as he grimaced from the burn of his drink.

He sat the glass down then said, "I got this. Calm down. You need to be handling Chase. He's our biggest threat." I rubbed my hands together as my mind started plotting out my next move.

Camille

Time to put things in motion, I thought. I still needed to lay low, but I knew that the weak link was Chase. He pretended like he had all his shit together, but he was like a kid. I would offer his ass some candy, and he would do whatever I commanded. At least that was what I was hoping for. After Steve was gone for the night, I made my way to his house. It was after one a.m., and he was not there. I guessed it was safer to find him at work, but tonight must not be the night for us to come together.

"Oh, my God," I thought out loud. What if Chase told Carlton that I was still pregnant? Would he be looking for me? Damn, that meant that I needed to watch my back. Damn, I needed some friends. Thank God I had some blackmail information. I remembered that I did have one friend, and I needed to see her. Searching my purse, I found my phone, then I texted the one friend that I had, requesting that they meet me at the Hilton.

Once I arrived at the Hilton, I got a room and sent the room number via text. I waited for my guest to arrive. Since there was no reply to my messages, I assumed that I would be spending the night alone. Forty-five minutes later, there was a knock at the door.

I opened the door, and there stood Monique. She was looking like a chocolate cupcake, wearing a trench coat. Please, sweet baby Jesus, let her be naked.

"Thank you for showing up. I know we haven't talked since our night with Carlton, but I would like to have that same type of fun."

She walked in the room, and she opened up her coat, exposing her perky breasts. A smile came across my face. Without hesitation, my hands started to caress her breasts. She let out a moan then grabbed my head and kissed me. I swore it was the best kiss I ever had. She started to massage my breast. Damn, I could not believe that I was about to have another encounter with a chick. Never in a million years would I do this. We broke the kiss and made our way to the bed. We were kissing and touching. I dared to stick the tip of my tongue out and briefly licked the inside of her upper lip.

I heard her breath catch, and she pulled slightly away from me, staring into my eyes for a split second. Then, with a groan, her mouth was on mine fully. Hot, wet, and open. Our tongues were meeting, tasting, then finally rubbing erotically against each other. I let out a small whimper, and her hand found its way to my neck, gently pulling me even closer. I thread my fingers through her hair and put my hand on the back of her head, keeping it there. I started sucking on her tongue, and it was as if a torrent was let loose. Both her hands were now on my shoulders, snaking their way down my back. Moaning wildly, she tossed one leg over me and quickly straddled my lap as if she'd been doing it for years. I knew this was permission to finally touch her the way I wanted to. I put my hands on her hips, squeezing and grabbing slightly. Still unable to get enough of each other's mouths, she pushed against me and rubbed her chest against my own. I felt every nerve ending on my hardened nipples. I held her by the waist, my thumbs grazing the underside of her breasts.

She let out a surprised "Oh!" and tossed her head back. I kissed and licked down her neck, my hand brave enough to gently cup her right breast over her. She moved away slightly, but I pulled her back forcefully and just held her for a moment. She looked up at me again. I saw that she was uncertain, and I knew then that she had never done this before. I couldn't promise to be gentle. I couldn't promise anything right now. I bent down for the kiss, and it was everything it should be. Her nails were digging into my lower back. She felt as though she was trying to push her entire body into mine, and then somehow, I really was pushing into her, my fingers filling her up, and she was crying out, gasping in surprise. Her forehead was pressed in my chest, and her fingernails pierced my flesh, drawing blood. She was hot, slick, and moving against me. She was so light that I was lifting her up with every thrust of my hand, and she was riding my fingers like the goddamn apocalypse was at hand.

I was fucking her as hard as I dared when suddenly, her heavy lids opened, and she was looking full and straight into my eyes. She bit me, my neck, my shoulder, before her warm mouth came to rest over my nipple which she nipped and suckled in turn. I could hardly control myself. I wanted to destroy her, I wanted to protect her, I wanted to own her, but most of all, I wanted to fuck her endlessly, keep this moment suspended in space and time. If I could somehow die right now and have this second be the apex of my life, I would willingly do so. I used one hand to restrain her, to hold her upright at the waist, as I moved back and kneeled. My fingers were still inside her, and she was begging me not to stop. She moaned as I helped her legs over my shoulders and spun her around so that her back was against the wall. I slowly rose until I was on my knees, and her feet were not touching the ground. From behind, my fingers were still resting in her, twitching only enough to keep her whimpering. My mouth was level with her clit now, and she was my captive. I licked her, sucked her, fucked her with my fingers while I pressed her against the wall and held her up with my other arm. I consumed her, utterly and completely. She thrusted her hips toward me, and my fingers were forced out as she rose her pelvis up and forward so that I had better access with my teeth and tongue. Her mouth was on my nipple again, teasing, licking, biting, flicking the hard tip of it with her tongue then almost taking my whole breast in her mouth.

"Mmmmm," she moaned into my body, and I felt it vibrate on my burning flesh.

"Oh, my God, Camille... This... feels... soooo good..." Her eyes were closed, her tongue still lavishing my breast. I barely even began to recognize the beginnings of an orgasm in my belly when it took me over. I was screaming and shaking and bucking against her hand. My orgasm was explosive and intense and had taken me completely by surprise. I looked at her face, and her eyes were wide, her mouth open, almost in disbelief that I was the one who had made her feel this way. I quickly crawled down and put my mouth on her clit, her fingers still pumping. It looked like she might blackout from the ecstasy. I slowed down as I felt her shaking from the orgasm. Her fingers were just inside me, her tongue licking me tenderly. I let out a long, soft "Aaahhh" and pulled her up to me, kissing her mouth and tasting my cum.

"Where... where..." I was still catching my breath. "Where did... you... learn to do... that..."

CHAPTER SEVENTEEN
Chase

I was losing my fucking mind, trying to find my fucking wife. Who the fuck had her? I had had my men stalking Camille's sister, and they were looking for Alexis. I reported her as a missing person. It was crazy. Her blood was found in Malone's car, and the internal affairs department was now involved. The blessing of being a cop was that they looked for your people faster. Of course, they were expecting that I had something to do with it. One of the guys for IA said that I killed Malone and Alexis because they were having an affair. "You sorry son of a bitch," was what I said before punching him in the face. That smug Black bastard. The commissioner told me to take some time off. At first, I was pissed, but it was exactly what I needed at this time, so I could get some personal shit in order.

After leaving the station, I went straight to the hospital, checking out the security camera. I was going to find Camille if it was the last thing that I did. Hours later, I finally found her ass, and she had a car. I wrote down the tag numbers and had one of my buddies report her new car stolen. Now, it was just a matter of time before I found that lying ass bitch.

Today had been a day from hell, and it was not over yet. There was still no word on Alexis or Camille. My grandmother said give everything to God, so I dropped down to my knees and prayed.

"Dear Lord, you say come as you are, and I am coming to you, asking for help. Please let my wife be okay and please help me find that bitch. Sorry, Lord, I meant find that chick, Camille, so I can kill her. In the name of Jesus, I pray. Thank you."

The only thing left to do was wait. Man, waiting was a fucking bitch. Just then, my cell rang.

"We found the bitch. She is at the Hilton downtown," Joe said.

Praying always works, I thought, not even replying, just heading to the hotel. A part of me wanted them to say that they had found my pregnant wife but no luck on her. Damn, Carlton was going to die for this shit. I swore on my fucking life. *Damn*, I thought as I pulled up to the Hilton.

While walking up to the hotel, there was a familiar face approaching the hotel. It was that stripper chick. Yes, she was going to lead me right to Camille. I quickly turned my back as she got closer. I didn't want her to recognize me and run. She made her way to the elevator, and I followed her. She got in and went to the tenth floor.

The girl walked in the room, and the door closed, echoing down the hall. A few moments later, I saw Carlton coming down the hall, once again turning my back. No one needed to see me there. Hopefully, I was out of range for the cameras, or I would have to make the evidence disappear. This was my chance to get rid of two problems at one time. Not to mention, I could start the takedown plan. As I made my way to the hotel room, I called in a tip about three drug houses. Since I had friends, I knew that the raids would take place. Not to mention, I said I heard my wife was hidden in one of the houses.

Time to start this war. I hoped these niggas were ready.

Wesley

The fact that Carlton had forced himself on my baby had me going crazy. I was trying to enjoy my time with her, but the only thing that I could think of was him on top of her. I was trying to hit it from the back. As soon as she started looking at me, I couldn't help but get pissed off.

"Carlton must die." I screamed at Chris.

"What's the plan, boss?" he questioned.

"I am thinking of one as we speak, but I am gonna have to come back to life."

"Boss, that is gonna be dangerous. How about you let me kill him?"

"No, Chris, this shit is personal! He tried to kill me, and he raped my girl."

"Awe, man, Wes, I did not know that. I am so sorry."

"It's all good. Is there anyone else in the clique that we can trust because I need more eyes and ears on the street?"

"Yeah, we can trust Big Tony."

I remembered that cat, Big Tony. He was a cool dude, but the number one question I had right now was could I trust his ass? I couldn't send Chris because Carlton would kill his ass on sight. Alexis waddled her ass down the steps. I couldn't bear to look her in the eyes. She flopped down on the couch next to Chris.

"Wesley, I am going home to Chase."

"No, the fuck you're not."

"Hear me out, Wesley. I go home, tell Chase what happened, and he kills Carlton, and we are in the clear. You stay dead, Chase goes to jail, and life is good."

"Alexis, you have to be out of your fucking mind to think that I am going to put my baby at risk."

"Wesley, stop being stubborn. This is the best way to go. How do you know that you can truly trust this Tony person? Yes, I listened at the steps. I know that you are going to do something stupid, and I want to help."

"No, Alexis, what you are going to do is sit your pregnant ass down."

She got up from the couch and stormed up the steps. I had to protect my family.

Carlton

Apartment 2-B was an extra apartment that my crew used for stashing money, drugs, and guns. I had never used it to torture someone, but I knew if I took him to the warehouse across town, people would notice.

"Keep your punk ass still before I drop your ass on the floor," grumbled Tony as the intruder flailed around like a slippery fish. As we got to the apartment doorway, Mike was still wiggling, so Tony just threw him on the carpeted floor. He came crashing down, making a loud thud sound as he laid, grimacing in pain, noticing his hands and feet were bound.

"What the hell you do that for?" I barked.

I looked at the guy who was writhing in pain as Tony laughed. "The motherfucker should've been still."

"You dumb motherfucker, you gonna draw attention," I added as Tony dragged the intruder into the apartment.

"Sit his bitch ass down," laughed Tony as he held a scalpel in his hand.

I loosened the tape on his mouth and asked again, "Are you ready to talk now?"

Before he could finish, Mike spat at him, laughed, and said, "I'm not telling you shit."

"You motherfucker," I said as I connected with an uppercut with so much force it dislocated his jaw and lifted the chair with him in it off the floor.

"UGHHHHHH," Mike whined as Tony re-taped his mouth as it was now swollen, and his jawbone was sticking out. The guy just rocked to deal with the pain.

"Let me get some of that," said Tony as he pulled the scalpel out. "Hold that nigga's head, Carlton." I braced his head as Tony took the scalpel and cut an incision at the intruder's eyelids, and he reached in his back pocket and poured some Visine into the incisions.

Tony stepped back as I pulled out the Desert Eagle and said, "I'm tired. He's not going to talk. Give me a potato out of my mini fridge."

Tony frowned at my comments and asked, "Now why the hell you got a potato in your mini fridge?"

Agitated, I answered. "Just give me the potato, smart ass."

"Hell, I'm pissed. I wanted to cut the nigga toes off," Tony replied.

"His bitch ass is working for Chase."

Mike grimaced with pain, but he knew the end was inevitable as I fixed the potato on the Desert Eagle and pressed it to his chest and squeezed two rounds into him. His body slumped immediately.

"I ain't cleaning up this mess," joked Tony.

I just shook my head.

"I guess cutting his toes off is out of the question?" Tony teased.

"I swear if you wasn't my dawg, I would put some heat in your ass too," I joked.

Tony frowned at the comment because my demeanor could be taken either way.

"Listen, round up the street team. We need to find Chris and get Alexis back," I added.

"We can't leave this body here," said Tony.

"Hello, this is Rafael." The man answered with a Russian accent.

"Hey, Rafael, where's Boris? I have a pickup job that needs to be handled asap," I said into my phone.

"What's the address, Carlton?" Rafael asked.

"The stash house in Piedmont Courts."

"Will there be any clean up involved?" he asked.

I looked at the floor and answered. "Yeah, light blood and urine where he pissed himself."

"I got a crew coming your way now," he responded. "Will this be cash or send you a bill?"

"Tell that dumb fuck, Rafael, to send me some Vodka," joked Tony.

Rafael paused then answered back, "Tell that fat cocksucker to come shine my shoes and bring me some chicken. Carlton, it's the usual thank you for your business as always. Oh, yeah, tell Tony to fuck himself," he said as he ended the call.

"Are you gonna be okay down here?" I questioned.

Tony scratched his head and answered. "Didn't you tell me we need to find Alexis? Now, how in the hell can I be two places at once?"

I didn't bother to answer. "I will send Nona down, so she can handle this. You come up when she relieves you, so we can roll out," I replied as I left.

Five minutes later, I was stepping off the elevator and saw Nona.

"Hey, I got a situation in 2-B I need you to handle," I said.

"I got you cause you always blessing me," Nona responded as she made her way to the elevator. Nona was a grimy crackhead who always did odd jobs for us.

***

We had been making all these moves, and things seemed to be falling in place. *There are two huge issues -*

Alexis and Camille, I thought while sitting back in my office, plotting my next moves, making a mental list of who all needed to be killed - Afon, Elle, Chase, and Alexis. I was ready to be the man on top. I had to get rid of anyone in my way. There was a soft knock on my door, breaking my thought process. Monique, one of my dancers, slowly walked in, smiling at me. Immediately, I thought back to the threesome I had with her and Camille.

"Sorry to bother you, boss, but I received a text message from Camille, asking me to meet up with her, and I know that you are looking for her, so I wanted you to know that we have her."

My night just got so much better.

"Good girl. Get sexy and go see her," I replied.

She walked out the door, no questions asked. The perfect little puppy. Hell, all women should be like her, just do what the fuck you said without any lip. I laughed as I made my way to my car.

Thirty minutes later, I was outside the Hilton, and so were three police cars. "Fuck," I yelled into my car as I watched Monique stroll across the street. She was wearing a coat, so a nigga wouldn't see what the fuck she had on under it. I got to the room, kicked the door in, fired shots, and here came the good guy cop messing up my night, and I didn't even know if I shot the bitch. I fired a few shots at Chase and ran around the corner, hiding in a room, hoping that Chase would come around, so I could put one in his head.

"Fuck," I yelled as I fired some shots at him then I hauled ass out of the hotel.

As soon as I get to my car, I got a text that said SWAT had hit three places.

Fuck my life, I thought as I called my lawyer.

Big Tony

I stayed around, keeping a vigilant watch to ensure the job was handled properly. Then, I gave Nona an extra hundred dollars for good measure, so she would keep her mouth shut. I walked Nona to the door. Then, I went in the bathroom and turned on the bathtub faucet full force and as hot as I could stand it. I went to the linen closet, grabbing the first towel I saw. As I took off my clothes, I remembered I needed to put the clothes I was wearing when Carlton killed Mike into the incinerator. So much shit had happened, and to make matters better, Carlton had made me his partner. Life was good.

It was an old wives' tale that in order to remain free from jail, one had to burn the clothes that you committed a crime in. I jumped into the tub and cringed a little from the heat. I was going to enjoy this bath. Next to jail house shower stalls, it was indeed a luxury. As soon as the thought hit that some bubbles would have been nice, Mysha came flying in the bathroom. Invading my space, she flipped open the lid and squeezed some of the liquid gel into the water. I waddled my arms in the water, trying to get the bubbles to increase. Me and Mysha giggled like two school aged children playing house when the babysitter wasn't looking.

"You like that, Daddy?" she asked me.

"Of course, bae, but can you do me a favor?" I started to say.

I had been with Mysha over ten years. I kept my home life and street life separate. I had lost a lot of things to the streets, including my son.

"I know already. Burn the damn outfit," Mysha said, reminding me neither one of us were new to the street life, which at times led us on a road to incarceration or death. We were glad our number didn't come up, thereby cutting the time we had together short. We were saddened by the loss of our loved ones. Some were so young they didn't even know what it meant to feel loved by anyone. Mysha's eyes moistened with tears as I knew she was thinking about our son we lost during one of Elle's Italian cartel's tumultuous street wars.

Our son, Case, was an innocent bystander of a bullet that was intended for me. Case was only three years old and a little spitting image of me. Mysha and I hadn't been the same since that fateful day. However, many people in the hood marveled at the fact that Mysha and I were still together, saying things like, 'relationships never last after the death of a child'.

I sensed something was wrong. When I looked up into Mysha's eyes, I didn't need to wonder or ask what the matter was. I could tell from her faraway look that she was thinking about Case. I was not really sure if I should break her out her trance and interrupt whatever emotion that she was experiencing. I just looked on as the different stages of pain registered on her face. I felt helpless that I couldn't comfort her when she had her zoned-out periods. That was when I forced her to talk in order to avoid her return to the dark recesses of her mind, which landed her three months in the psych ward to cope with the loss of Case.

"Bae, I'm here. Talk to me," I spoke up gently, coaxing her back to our present surroundings. It hurt that I was always on my grind and couldn't be here for her. I loved her with all of my being because she was my day one when I didn't have a pot to piss in or the window to throw it out of.

"Oh, sorry. For a moment, I thought of little man. I saw him wrapped in all white with wings like a dove. I thought God would allow me to hold him for a moment," Mysha stated. I gave her a pass when she rambled nonsense like this. I just listened without any judgement.

My heart strings pulled and tugged in a million different directions. I hated to even think of the death of our child, Case, my first born son. Mysha and I tried for a little over a year to have another child without much success. I brought up the matter of adoption to Mysha, and she wasn't too thrilled. She felt that although all children deserved to be loved, she needed to love her own like she did the one who was so violently taken away from her. In my heart of hearts, I really couldn't argue with her logic because I genuinely felt the same way. I only offered the option of adoption to pull her out of the pain she was waddling in, the pain we both struggled with daily.

"Mysha, listen to me. I need you to listen to me real good now. Your vision, or visions rather, simply are a sign from God that it's okay to let go of some of your pain because Case is safe with him. He's with God now and all our loved ones that passed on before and after him. God was just allowing you a glimpse of our angel to help you put away your pain. Case feels no pain because he's safe from the turmoil and hell on Earth that he would have had to face with parents in this lifestyle. Do you understand what you saw, baby?" I pleaded with every fiber of my being for Mysha to come to grips that things were changed, but we still had to move on and that our little soldier wasn't suffering or feeling any type of discomfort.

I had always carried the burden of Case's death in the back of my mind. It was the worst pain I had ever felt because the same streets that I loved took my only son's life.

I had been constantly grinding as always. It was a Saturday evening, I and had taken Case to the old neighborhood as usual to get his haircut and to hangout. Gunfire suddenly erupted as we made our way down the sidewalk. Kareem and his crew drove by, spraying at whatever moved. I knew I was his prime target. He always had a certain disdain for me taking Mysha away from him. The fact that she gave me a child was like salt in an open wound for him. Kareem's goons had scoped out mine and Case's every move that day. Plus, he wanted to take from Mysha what he knew mattered most to her... Case. He knew that she loved me, but Case was her heart, soul, and her drive.

"Hey, motherfucker, it's judgement day," he yelled as they drove by, spraying the sidewalk with rounds.

I grabbed Case as rounds flew everywhere, taking a few hits as I shielded Case. Case had taken a direct hit unbeknownst to me, and I had taken one round in the back and two rounds in the torso. After they drove off, Case's limp body was like that of a rag doll in my arms. Case's body was

CAUGHT UP IN A THUG'S LOVE

now cold as ice. The impact of bullets had riddled cars, people, and houses in its path.

"Case... Case," I yelled as the adrenaline pumped through my body.

Slugs burned deep in my body as I fought for consciousness. I heard the sirens blaring in the background as blood leaked from Case's mouth. That was the last thing I remembered as the darkness of unconsciousness finally took over.

Me and Mysha both snapped out of our trances. We decided a long time ago that blaming each other for the war with Kareem and little Case's death would only push us farther apart. We planned to live a long, healthy life together. Although no other child could replace Case, the child would be a symbol of how far we've come in healing. I climbed out of the tub as Mysha held a large beige towel open so that she may assist in drying me off. As I stepped out the tub, she pushed my slippers closer to me so that my feet wouldn't touch the bare floor. This was another factor I loved about her. She was attentive to my every need without seeming desperate. She had a natural submissiveness to her, not to be mistaken for being a weak woman.

I almost slipped and grabbed onto her shoulder for reassurance. She quickly grasped my lower arm.

"Whoa there, Daddy. I got you. Now lift up your leg and let me dry you off," she said, smiling as she pampered me.

I did as I was instructed, loving every bit of tenderness from Mysha. When it was all said and done, my dick was at full attention. Mysha laughed and swiped at it with her hand.

"Not right now, soldier. Stand down." She giggled and turned to walk out the bathroom. I grabbed her from behind and held onto her tightly, not wanting to ever let go. I nestled my head into her neck then whispered ever so gently, "You do know I love and miss our child, don't you?"

Mysha was instantly taken aback and somewhat angry. She didn't want to discuss my feelings right now. It seemed to her that she always did and discussed everything pertaining to me. Then, when it was time for her to feel or go through something, I would always tell her to instantly get over it. This was becoming a norm in her life. It seemed everyone wanted her to be their superwoman without being there for her. She always thought that the worst part of being strong was that no one expected her to have weak moments. It was in these moments that she didn't need to worry about anyone else's love for her child. She loved her child and because of me and the rest of the team's greed, her child was no longer walking this Earth but was an angel.

Mysha shrugged me off of her and proceeded to walk out the bathroom while calling out to me.

"Yeah, yeah, I know. You loved Case more than anyone. I think I get it. I'm going to take a nap now. I just became tired!"

I thought to myself things had better change soon. She needed me to control her feelings just a little more when it came to talking about Case. I just sighed. I knew I had fucked up, plus now with Wesley's death, becoming Carlton's partner and right-hand man, I was going to be busy. Not to mention, I was trying to find Alexis. This shit only kept me away from home more. I hated to leave with us at odds, but it paid for our lifestyle.

Plus, Carlton did business with the Italians who killed my kid, and I would get revenge on the evil bitch.

Alexis

Wesley had me completely fucked up if he thought that I was going to sit around and let his crazy ass cousin kill him. I would not stand for that. I locked the door so that Wesley could not get in the room. As soon as they fell asleep, I was going to go home to my husband. If I could get him and Carlton to kill each other, it would be perfect.

Three hours later, I quietly opened the bedroom door and crept down the steps. Wesley was on the couch, and his ass slept too light for me to get out the front door. Tiptoeing down the hall, I searched for the backdoor, and I found it. I grabbed his car keys. They were by the door, and I was free. Once in the car, I started the engine and took off, praying that he didn't hear me. Five hours later, I was home, and there was no sign of Chase. I picked up the house phone and called his cell.

He answered on the first ring.

"Hello."

"Chase, baby, I need you. I'm at home."

"I'll be there in a few minutes."

Good job, Chase. Be the sweet, loving husband that I knew you were not. Fifteen minutes later, the door opened. He stared at me then ran over, throwing his arms around me.

"What the fuck happened to you?"

"Where do I start, Chase?"

"At the beginning."

"Carlton kidnapped and raped me, then I got away from him and ran to the bus station so that I could get out of town because I am scared that he will kill me. He hates me. Then, Malone kidnapped and beat me. He attempted to sell me to Carlton. Then, Carlton shot him in the head, and as he was trying to kidnap me, one of his friends tried to save me. I asked him nicely to let me go, and he did out of respect for Wesley."

Chase turned gray as he took in all that I had said to him. He looked at me as tears flowed from my eyes. I was truly sad. The last place I wanted to be was with Chase right now.

"Babe, I am so sorry that this happened to you. I swear Carlton will pay for what he has done to us."

"Chase, he is dangerous, plus you can't just kill him."

"Alexis, I need you safe, so get some clothes. I have to get you out of here."

"Where are we going?"

"Just get some things."

227

I got off the couch and walked to the bedroom and grabbed us both a few things. Moments later, we were out the door and on the road.

Hours later, we arrived at a large, brick house. It was beautiful. Chase hopped out the car, running around to my side of the car, opening the door to let me out the car.

"Welcome home, baby."

"When did we buy this, and how can you afford this on a cops' salary?"

"Alexis, don't be a reporter. Just enjoy what we have. You go in the house, and I will go grab us some dinner."

Chase handed me some keys and watched me walk to the door. I got inside the house and locked the door behind me. I had no phone and no way to get in touch with Wesley. This was surely not a smart idea.

CHAPTER EIGHTEEN

Chase

I was at the hotel spectating and trying to find out if Camille was dead. From what I could gather, two people were rushed to the hospital, but the news did not release the names of the victims. *Fuck*, I thought to myself when I got a call from my house phone. Who the hell was calling me from my house? It was Alexis. Yes, my baby was home, and I was happy to see her. She told me that Carlton had her kidnapped. I was going to kill that son of a bitch! The best thing was that I was able to take her to our new home. No one knew that she was not missing, so after I treated her real good, if she acted like she wanted to leave me, I would blow her fucking brains out. She had a few days to tell me that she still loved me. Our wedding vows said until death do us part, and I took that shit to heart.

While I was on my way to get my baby some food, I got a call from an unknown number.

"What?" I answered.

"When you play pussy, you get fucked, white boy. I hope you said goodbye to your sweet mom. I sure did as I put two bullets in her old ass. Alexis is next, but that bitch, I am gonna fuck a few more times before I cut her throat. I plan to do it all while you watch."

"If you hurt my momma, boy, I will kill you."

The line went dead, and I started to call my mother frantically. There was no answer. I called my department and asked them to stop by her house. Three minutes later, I got a call that confirmed that my mom was in fact dead.

My heart fell to the floor as my heart shattered. I grabbed Alexis's food and went back to the house. I made it inside and collapsed at the door.

Wesley

It was almost ten a.m., and I had not heard Alexis come out the room, not one time. Hell, I thought that pregnant women had to pee all the time. Damn, I needed to apologize to her ass and get her somewhere safe.

I got up and headed to the steps and saw that the bedroom door was open. I walked in and no Alexis. There was a piece of paper on the bed. I picked it up and read it, instantly pissed.

Wes,

Please don't be mad. I had to do this for us. You need to stay in the clear. Be dead until we are able to be with each other. Please trust me on this one. I can handle Chase. After I tell Chase what happened, he will handle Carlton, and we both will have clean hands.

I love you so much,

Alexis.

Damn, I thought as I sat on the bed. It was time to do some shit that you only saw on TV. I needed a makeup artist that could give me a new face. I was going to save my family. I had one little chick that I used to fuck with back in the day. I hit her up and asked her to give me a new face. She said it would take some time, but she had me. I couldn't wait to see what she came up with.

I took out the phone and tried to call the burner phone that I had given Alexis, and the sound of the vibrating phone came from the nightstand. Alexis better pray that Carlton didn't get her before I did because she was doing some stupid ass shit.

Camille

I woke up to a lot of beeping and tubes everywhere. I looked around to see that I was in the hospital. I could not move the lower part of my body, and I started to panic. Alarms started to go off, and a team of nurses rushed in the room, telling me to calm down. Two of them held down my arms, and I cried.

"Camille, calm down," someone yelled.

I looked to the right and saw Carlton sitting in the corner.

"Get him out of here," I cried.

"Camille, that is not a smart idea. We need to talk."

I looked at my stomach, and it was gone. "What the fuck happened to my baby?" I cried.

"That is why we need to talk, Camille." Carlton demanded.

The nurse gave me a sad look. She dropped her head and started to say, "I am so sorry that you..."

Then, Carlton interrupted her by firmly saying, "Thank you, nurse. You can leave now."

She looked at him as if she was going to say something, but she looked at me as if she knew I was scared out of my mind. After she was gone, Carlton approached the bed and sat in the chair closest to me.

"Camille, honey, you did not keep your end of the bargain. I said that I would spare your life if you got rid of the baby, and you didn't. Camille, you played me, and I ended up killing my best stripper trying to kill you. For that you need to pay. Luckily, I shot you in the stomach, and you lost the baby."

Tears poured from my eyes as I started to struggle to catch my breath. "Why are you such an evil person?"

"Camille, you have forty-eight hours to end your life."

"You better go ahead and kill me because I will not take my own life. So, you better shoot me now."

He burst into laughter, then between clenched teeth, he said, "Bitch, I will blow your fucking brains out. You have forty-eight hours. Do it yourself or I will do it for you."

Carlton walked out the room, giving me a big smile. I smiled back because this nigga was going to have to catch my Black ass first.

Twenty minutes after he left, I pressed the button for the nurse to come in, and I told her that I needed to get out of here. I had no friends or family to help me. I cried so that she could know that I was genuinely scared that he would kill me. I told this little white lady that I was scared he would make me a sex slave, and I convinced her that he was paying the cops. She said that she was going to help me. The next day, some ladies from the women's center were there to take me away from my abusive boyfriend. Carlton better know that I was coming for his punk ass, and I was going to come hard.

Big Tony

Damn, Carlton was playing with fire, and I was not sure if I wanted to be in his crew. I was usually ride or die, but this mothafucker had me follow him to a lick. He killed a defenseless old ass lady. I mean, for real, this lady had to be in her nineties, and he shot her twice, recorded the shit, and then had his crew deliver it to Chase's house.

I was a ruthless motherfucker, but it broke my heart watching that shit. I had my main goal, and that was to take down the Italians, and after that, I was going to just chill and get out this game. I just needed to avenge my son's death.

I was sitting on my couch, smoking a blunt, when my phone rang.

"What?" I answered, trying to figure out who the hell was calling me.

"Bruh, this is Chris. I need your help."

"Why should I help you? Yo ass left me in the middle of nowhere."

"Because we blood, nigga, and not to mention, your boy, Carlton, is out of control. He needs to be stopped, and I think that we can take him down."

He was right. He was a loose cannon, and Chris was my brother, so I had to have his back. Plus, I needed to figure out why he suddenly wanted to take Carlton down.

He told me that we would meet next week, and I was cool. We needed to meet. Me and my brother could take over the streets. Carlton was on some foul shit. The shit he was doing was reckless. I mean, this nigga expected me to follow him on that bullshit. Man, I was missing my nigga, Wesley. He was more rational.

Days Later...

Wesley

The make-up artist did her thing. My face was the fucking shit. I was on my way back to North Carolina. The first thing I needed to do was find Alexis. I needed her and my baby to be safe. Then, I had to meet with Carlton. My plan was to make him think that I was a supplier. I knew that he would jump on this because he was greedy, but I would talk to Afon first to ensure that he would take the deal. Chris was supposed to talk to his brother, Tony, and see if he could help us take down Carlton. I hoped that we could trust his brother because I didn't want to have to kill Chris.

A few hours later, I was back home, and I had no clue how the fuck I was going to find Alexis. Just as I was getting settled into my hotel, I heard on the news that Chase's mom was murdered, and the funeral would be today. Lady Luck was on my side. I attended the funeral and at the repast finally saw Alexis alone. I approached her. She was looking at me crazy. Since I was wearing my mask, I just gave her an envelope. In it was a phone, and I was going to call her. I waited around and followed her and Chase to a place in Charlotte. Once I found out where they lived, I called Chase's cell phone, blocking my number, telling him that I had details about his mother's death. I knew that would get him out of the house. He ran out the house like fire was on his ass.

That was my chance to see Alexis. As soon as he was gone, I called her.

"Hello."

"I should kick your ass, walking out on me. Having me worried out my mind."

"Wes?"

"Yes, and I want to see you. Come outside so we can talk," I demanded.

Without arguing, she came out the house, looking pretty as she waddled to her car, smiling at me. We got in, and she pulled off. She looked uncomfortable in the BMW as we drove down to the park below Chase's house. After we parked, I noticed her motherly glow. The shit turned me on knowing my seed was the reason for it.

"Babe, you need to be in a safe place if Carlton is killing people that Chase loves."

"I know. That is why we are here."

"You see how easy it was for me to find you, Alexis. I mean really," I fussed.

Her head dropped to the ground, and tears poured out her eyes. I was pissed at the fucked-up decisions she was making.

"What happened to your face?" she asked in between her sobbing.

"C'mon, baby. Every thug, low life, and hit man in Charlotte probably looking for me," I answered. "I need your hard-headed, pregnant ass to get back to the spot. I have some moves I need to make," I fumed.

"So, you think Carlton or Afon behind this?" asked Alexis as I read the concern on her face.

"I don't know, baby. All I know is you're carrying my fucking seed. Your ass needs to take a fucking seat."

I was pissed that her ass ended up with Chase, but I at least knew she was safe seeing he was the chief of police.

"I need you to quit treating me like I'm some helpless ass chick," she snapped.

I grimaced at her comments, wanting to snatch her little ass up. I gave her a pass.

"Let me be clear. I need your ass to stay put. Let me handle this shit. Do you understand?" I fussed as she rolled her eyes but agreed.

"Stop talking to me like you're my daddy." She again frowned, rolling her eyes.

"Don't make me put some hot shit in your ass. You better not be letting that clown touch you," I growled.

"Boy, bye with that shit. I'm only with Chase for the fact that I know you're taking care of business. Chill the fuck out," explained Alexis. Alexis was now pissed as she pouted. I had simmered down, knowing I had to keep a leveled head. "Okay, I have to get back because Chase has officers patrolling the house," she added.

"That's the least his punk ass can do. I need you to play your part," I fussed.

I could tell she wanted to say something slick, but she didn't.

I pulled her to me as I tongued her little sassy ass down. She melted in my arms. She was my reason for living. As much as she was a pain in my ass, she was my peace. I needed her like a camel needed water.

"Whew, damn, you kissed me like I will never see you again," Alexis responded when I released her.

"Never that! You know I beat these streets," I bragged.

I saw the tears swelling up in her eyes. I needed her to be at ease and focus on the baby while I handled this shit with Carlton.

"Calm down, baby. I got to roll out," I assured her.

She pulled me in for an embrace before I hopped out of her car. I knew I would need to form alliances to be able to get at Carlton's bitch ass. I looked back and winked at her as I walked back to my Range Rover.

CHAPTER NINETEEN
Big Tony

I had to admit I wouldn't take my brother out for anyone. He was the only remnant of family I had besides Mysha. Yeah, I knew Carlton was on some grimy shit. I just didn't realize it was this deep. Me and Chris both saw he was a snake. We were down for Wesley.

"Word, bro. Carlton on some devious shit," I said as I turned right into a deserted parking lot.

"I always felt like that nigga was jealous of Wesley," responded Chris. I searched the parking lot. I noticed a blue work van that I had being seeing frequently lately. Something about the driver side caught my eye. I put Chris on alert as I reached under the seat and pulled out my .45.

"Wassup, bruh?" questioned Chris as he was now cocking his 9mm.

"I been seeing that van a lot lately," I answered.

"Let's roll up on these motherfuckers. See wassup," said Chris as he took the safety off.

"Damn, bro, so Wesley's ass is alive?" I asked.

"Yeah, that nigga wants Carlton with a passion," Chris added.

"Chris, shut the hell up," I said, shocked at the fact that Carlton would shit on his blood over petty shit like he was doing. "We will finish that conversation later."

"Who you think these lame asses are in this vehicle?" asked Chris.

"Hell, they might be Chase's boys undercover," I responded. "I don't want this white boy getting nervous and taking off, so I'm trying not to make any sudden movements," I said.

My plan was to throw the .45 in his face and see what the fuck he wanted with us. "You know them white boys don't play. They will kidnap you and eat your whole family. Hence all those damn serial killers - Dahmer, Gacy, Bundy, Manson, and the list goes on."

"Hmmm-hmmm. Whatever, just be careful. You know there's cameras everywhere," warned Chris.

"You hold on for a moment. I don't even know how many are in this damn van. When you see me throw the gun in his face then you reach under the seat for mine. I might need a backup piece if there's more than one in that vehicle," I commanded Chris.

"Alright, bro-bro. You got it. I'll have your back. Fuck these punk white boys," Chris said.

I looked at my brother and burst out laughing. I thought to myself that he was probably the craziest one out of all of our siblings. The one who was a true right hand. Regardless of if he left me to save Alexis, it was all good.

I then slowly whispered to him, "I'll be right back," as I got out of the car. I stooped down real low and gangster bopped to the blue van. I popped up just in time to see the driver of the van reaching for a weapon.

"Huh-huh, homeboy. Remove your hand off that steel or get two to the dome asap," I demanded of the driver.

I continued to speak after being entirely sure that my enemy's hand was off the weapon, and the coast was clear of impending danger. "Now, what the fuck are you doing around these parts, and who sent you?" I snapped.

"Of course, you'd like to know, Tony. Isn't that what your crew call you, homie?" the driver retorted to me, showing no traces of fear.

I cringed at the sound of the man's voice and the way he tried to be hard, knowing his ass was at death's door. Even if this driver did have a valid reason for following us, I was determined to use him for target practice, just to sharpen up my skills if he didn't talk. I signaled for Chris to cover me. Once he covered me, I made my way to the passenger side of the blue van and slid in. I turned around in my seat, gun drawn, looking for any signs of a possible kidnapping. I didn't find any but didn't exactly let the driver off easily. "Bruh, just kill his ass since he's so hard," teased Chris, and in turn, the driver grimaced.

"Baby bruh, call Mysha's phone and see if she answers. If and once she does, tell her you're just checking on her. I need to know if she's safe or not," I instructed my brother. He kept the gun steady on our intended victim, waiting for signs of a confirmation that Mysha was alive and well. That confirmation came shortly after Mysha answered the phone.

As he ended the call, his only words were simply, "Finish him."

I smiled, knowing Mysha was okay. I always worried about her, even though she could take care of herself.

"Don't make any sudden moves or hand signals to other cars. Now, turn around and drive the speed limit until you get to Westchester Road then make the left and go the back roads until you find your way hitting Concord," I demanded my hostage.

Our hostage shook his head, indicating an understanding of my instructions. I braced myself as the van started to crawl at a slow pace. Keeping a vigilant eye on the driver, my senses went up, surveying the outside surroundings as well. As the vehicle turned right on Westchester Road and Gun Hill Road, I told the driver to speed it up.

"I know he said drive at a slow pace by doing the speed limit, but a pregnant dog moves faster than this shit here. Speed it up, why don't ya?" complained Chris.

"Listen, man, you know I'm Chase's right hand, don't you? What do you think is going to happen to you when he finds out I'm maimed or dead or something? You think he's going to let it ride?" the driver pleaded.

"Aye, stop all that blubbering. Your death will be quick and painless. Now, I know you don't want word to get out that you started begging like a bitch begs for the dick coming off their periods or what? Or do you want to die like a man by telling me to go fuck myself?" I asked while giggling to myself.

The wait was the best part of taking a motherfucker's life. I loved the look on his face as the fact registered that death was certainly imminent and that I was the one who was going to send him to his maker. I continued to pour salt into the driver's wound by asking his name. When informed it was Frank, Chris starting clowning on him even harder.

"I was tailing you hoping to get a lead on Wesley," explained Frank. "Chase has a hunch he isn't dead."

"Last I heard was that Wesley was dead," I lied. I watched as Frank's face was suddenly whitewashed, knowing that his explanation didn't help.

"Say, Frankie baby, I can't wait to tell everyone about Chase's hitta that shitted on himself," I exclaimed as he sniffed the air and saw a brown stain forming on the driver's seat next to him.

"I thought you were a gangster. I never figured Chase would have a bitch ass dude for a right hand. A right hand that would shit on himself at the first sign of trouble. I bet he is just a bitch ass himself," I bragged. "Matter of fact, Chase is a bitch ass nigga. From the time he lost his woman, I could tell he wasn't nothing but a bitch who barked orders. Pull into that field over there by the highway exit, so we can get this over with," I ordered.

"About fucking time," chimed Chris, who was slightly annoyed.

"Listen, you really don't want to do this. Our paths crossed by chance," begged Frank.

Frank was horrified when I raised the gun directly toward his temple. I could tell he thought he would have had more time to plead or bargain his way out. However, he realized just how wrong he was when he pulled off into the field. I let off the first shot as it pierced through his skull.

Brains, skull, and flesh flew everywhere, covering the seats, window, and dashboard. I removed the muzzle of the gun and whispered, "Oh, well, shit happens." I looked around when something in the rearview windshield caught my attention. It was Mysha's Chevy. My heart dropped, hoping that Frank didn't have a partner who captured my lady. I tried to sneak out of the van as unnoticeably as possible when Chris ran up and opened the passenger's side door of the van very quickly and even more widely. "How the fuck did she know where we were?" I questioned out loud. By this time, she was walking towards the van. "How the hell you find us?" I barked.

"I GPS'ed you off of the tracker I have installed in your phone," she answered, noticing the mess Frank had made. I grimaced at the fact that she was tracking me. "So, you gonna sit here all day and fuck around and get caught or move your ass?" she joked. I couldn't respond.

"Let's go, big bro-bro. Mysha and I got you," Chris assured me. I jumped in Mysha's car, so we could drop Chris back at his car.

"You two are my world. No one has better hittas that could handle a nigga the way you two do," I said, stroking Chris and Mysha's egos when all of a sudden, gunshots rang out from the distance. I looked out of the window. It seemed to be a cement truck. Mysha screamed out.

"Oh, shit, hit the gas,"

"Nah, Daddy. You and Chris get fire off those cannons while I hit the gas."

Chris and I were both in the backseat. I shot out the back window as Mysha sped off, jumping on the highway, heading farther into Concord with the cement truck advancing fast on our tail.

"Who the fuck is shooting at us?" I wondered out loud as Mysha punched the Camaro's gas pedal all the way to the floor.

"Who the hell is shooting at us?" Chris asked in the same instant as me.

I looked at Chris and pointed my finger while giving a head nod. "Great minds, great minds." The two of us laughed as if there weren't any impending danger speeding towards us to the point Mysha had to cut in.

"Now that that's established, can you make us ghost? I still have a little living I'd like to do, but we got to get away from that damn cement truck," yelled Mysha.

Mysha drove like she never drove before. To the average Joe, they would have thought Mysha was a trained professional. She caught every curve of the road with precision. With the truck on our bumper, she acted quickly to do something to shake the truck.

"Fuck this. Give me an angle for a shot," yelled Chris as he lined up with the truck.

"Hold up. Let me hit this U-turn and pick whoever's ass off," yelled Mysha.

Chris was now hanging out of the window, letting off rounds. "Blam, blam, blam." As fire streamed from the barrel, the truck swerved left to avoid the shots that Chris let off. The truck caught the side of some parked car, which the impact crushed like aluminum cans. Mysha had put distance between us with the distraction and had enough time to let me out. I ran to the passenger side while the truck tried to unhinge itself from the bumper of an old Plymouth Volare. The driver was so involved in getting the truck loose that he didn't notice me stepping on the passenger sideboard with my .45 in hand as the big truck thrashed back and forth. Mysha had now parked the Camaro.

"Hey, buddy," I yelled to distract the driver as Chris came on the driver side and crashed the window with the butt of his 9mm.

The driver was focused on me till he heard the window shatter. "What the fuck?" he muttered. "Get the fuck away from this truck." He tried to reach for his snub nose .38 that was on the seat.

As he did so, Chris jumped to give me a clear shot. "Kabloom! Kabloom!" The driver slumped over in the seat, and the truck came to a rest.

"What the fuck?" I sighed. Chris and Mysha were shook from what happened. The fact that someone came for me had a nigga paranoid, plus I knew I now had to watch my back for Chase and Carlton.

"Hey, is everybody cool?" I asked, and they both nodded their heads. "Hey, bruh, heat is on. But tell Wesley I'm down to get Carlton's punk ass," I told him as we dropped him back at his car.

"He already know you down, bruh," responded Chris as he got into his car. "Bye, sister-in-law. Hell of a job driving." We waved as Mysha pulled off.

Wesley

Leaving Alexis at Chase's house had me feeling some type of way for real. It was time to put an end to this shit! I took off my make-up. It was time for the streets to know that Wesley was fucking alive.

As I walked past the front desk, my eyes were met by Cierra's bright smile. "Good evening, Mr. Wesley."

"Good evening. How are you today?" I asked.

I had been staying at the Blake in downtown Charlotte. I knew I would need Elle's unstable ass on my team, so I reached out to her to discuss what was going on. Cierra was the flirty desk clerk who was sweating a nigga's swag.

"I am fine," she answered.

I turned and looked at her and took in the way her uniform made her ass bulge out like it had the mumps. "Damn," I said to myself as she purposely poked her ass out.

"How was your weekend?" I asked sarcastically, playing off the fact that she caught me peeping at her ass.

Cierra winked and said, "One of the best I've had in years."

"That's good. Mine wasn't too bad either," I responded. "Well, nice talking with you. I didn't get much sleep last night. About to go get me a nap," I interjected.

"I hope you get some rest. You look tired," Cierra replied.

"I hope so too. I really need it," I responded as I made my way to the elevator. "Well, enjoy your day," I added before stepping on the elevator.

I was skeptical about fucking with Elle. Chris had called and told me that he had schooled Big Tony on the foul shit that Carlton was on.

I got off the elevator and turned towards my room, which was about midway down the hall. I could immediately detect something was different as I pulled out the room key. It was a fragrance that I had smelled before.

"Where have I smelled that scent before?"

I unlocked the door and discovered Elle dressed in a blue and black panty set with thigh high stockings.

"Wassup?" I asked, dropping the room key on the desk.

Elle smiled mischievously. "Nothing. Just waiting on you. So, what's up with you?"

I was flattered, but at the same time, the lack of sleep from the night before was demanding my attention. I smiled. "Baby, I am really tired, but if you want to practice, we can."

Elle was glad that her gesture was well received. "I figured we had the rest of the day to ourselves so..."

I remained diplomatic as she answered. "So, what do you have in mind?"

Elle's face lit up with my response. "Well, I figure we can enjoy one another's company and go from there," she responded.

I replied. "Sounds like one hell of a plan to me. Well, let me take a shower first."

Elle was lying on the bed, looking at a magazine when she asked, "Do you need some company?"

I smiled. "See, now you being bad." I started to get undressed and ready for the shower.

Elle watched as I carefully removed my clothes. "Take your time. I am taking in the view," Elle remarked.

I was now naked as I stood in front of Elle.

I laughed as her eyes lit up at the sight of my body and the way my limp dick hung with a curve. "I will be right back," I said as I made my way to the shower.

Elle's pussy was demanding her attention as I showered. She laid back on the bed as she unclasped the teddy at the crotch which was moist from the heat coming from her pussy. I peeped before getting into the shower. She gently slid a finger in her pussy for lubrication as she slid her fingers across her clit. She purred as her fingers gently massaged it as the tip was swollen.

She flicked at it as she rubbed it back and forth and moaned, "Ummm, wwwweeehhhh," as she took light breaths as the intensity of the pleasure was increasing. Her eyes were shut as she was caught up in pleasuring herself.

"Oooo, fucckk," she repeated as her fingers dipped in and out of her pussy. Her juices lathered her fingers.

Her face grimaced as she lightly bit her lip. "Ummm," she groaned as the strokes of her fingers moved faster. As she was nearing climax, I was walking back into the room.

"You need some help with that?" I asked.

Elle was startled as she snapped back to reality and answered seductively. "I can always use a helping hand."

I walked over to the bed and grabbed her by her legs and pulled her to the edge of the bed, so I would be eye level to her pussy. I opened her legs as I licked the insides of her thighs. She cooed as my tongue ran up and down her leg.

"Sssss," was the only sound that escaped her lips as I worked my way up to the lips of her pussy.

I took my thumb and pulled the pussy as I teased her swollen clit. I flicked my tongue at the wetness inside of them. Elle's head was tilted back as my tongue ran up and down the sides of her clit. I teased her, never directly letting my tongue touch her clit.

"Damn, damn," she moaned as her head ground into the pillow it was resting on.

Her hand gripped at the bed sheets as if she was trying to pull them off. Her legs trembled at every lap of my tongue. Her stomach quivered from the pleasure my tongue was sending through her body. Her eyes were closed as slight streams of tears rolled down her face.

"Come on, baby. Don't tease me like this," Elle moaned.

I then ran my tongue from the top to the bottom of her clit gently as her body rocked with intensity. She clawed at the sheets even more as she bit her lip.

"Right there, right there," escaped her lips as my tongue wildly licked at her clit.

I groaned as I buried my face into her pussy.

"Whew, whew, whew," escaped her lips as her body was being drained by the orgasm that seemed like it lasted five minutes.

I raised my head after she had reached her climax. The bed was wet from the explosion.

"Mmmmm... mmmmm," she whispered hoarsely.

I smiled as I looked at her. "You okay?" I teased.

Elle laid exhausted from the episode. "You got me," she muttered as she waved me away.

Her statement stroked my ego as I joked, "I told you that you weren't ready."

"Whatever," she purred as she was dozing off.

"Look at you, I put that ass to sleep," I joked as I smacked her on the ass. I cuddled up next to her as we allowed the feather top mattress to consume us while we slept. I knew me fucking around on Alexis was fucked up, but sometimes, you had to do things you hated to protect the ones that you loved. Alexis was carrying my seed. I knew I needed to do whatever it took to make sure that Alexis was good. She was my reason for living. But the one thing her ass was not going to do was leave me. I would kill her before I let anyone have her, especially that white boy.

***

I hit up Chris and told him and Big Tony to meet me at the hotel so that we could come up with a plan and make our moves. About thirty minutes later, there was a knock on the door. I let Chris and Tony in.

They sat on the couch. I started off by saying, "The enemy of my enemy is my friend." They looked at me, confused.

"Big Tony, I need you to be one hundred percent down with me, and I swear you will reap the benefits. But you have to trust me."

"I trust you," Big Tony replied. As soon as the words left his mouth, there stood Elle.

He gave her a death look, and I quickly started to talk.

"Elle is going to be our main supplier, and she is no longer doing business with Carlton. We have to cut off his money in order to take over the streets."

Elle nodded her head and gave a flirty smile before saying, "Yes, I am about to get out of here and end things tonight."

She smiled at me before walking out the door.

Chris, Tony, and I sat there in silence. Big Tony went to speak, but I put my finger up. Then, I sent them a text message saying that we couldn't talk here. We needed to go for a ride. In sync, we all walked out the room together. I was shocked to find that Elle was waiting outside the door, trying to listen. Since Elle had access to the room before I had gotten there, I didn't want to take a chance that the room had been bugged. We ended up going to Big Tony's house.

He walked in before Chris and I. Once we were in, Big Tony said, "I refuse to work with that bitch."

"Look, Tony, at this time, we need her. We have to keep our enemies close. Once Carlton is dead, we can take her ass out, and we can own the streets."

The last thing I had to do was make a personal appearance to Afon to let him know that I was alive. I walked to his house, and his guards looked as if they were going to shit themselves once they laid eyes on me. When I walked in, he was sitting at the table. He stood up, walking towards me.

"Lazarus has risen," he said, laughing.

"Yes, and it's time to kill some snakes."

He extended out his arms, giving me a big hug.

"I'm happy to see you, Wesley," he stated, then he punched me in the chest, knocking the wind out of me. "Don't you ever do that shit again."

Once the air was back in my chest, I replied. "Sorry. I needed everyone to assume I was dead."

He gave me a head nod, and I told him about my plan to take down Carlton. I told him how I fucked Elle, and I knew she would be on my side. I knew that he didn't approve of that because his facial expression showed his disgust.

CHAPTER TWENTY

Chase

Nothing could have prepared me for what I had just heard on the phone. As soon as I said hello, a fellow officer said that Frank had been found dead. "Damn!" I yelled, throwing the house phone into the wall. Alexis came running into the living room.

"Are you okay?" she questioned.

"Frank is dead."

"I am so sorry," she said, throwing her arms around me. In the last forty-five days, I had lost both my best friends and my mother. *Can shit get any worse?* I thought to myself. Just as I said that, there was a knock on the door. Alexis broke our embrace, and she went to open the door. No one should have known where we were. I stood up, reaching for my gun. I heard a man's voice, then I heard Alexis say, "This is a bad idea."

Moments later, Wesley waltzed into the room.

This night officially got worse. I pointed my Glock at him, and he smiled at me.

"Look, white boy, I didn't come here to kill you. I actually came in peace. We have a problem that we need to eliminate together."

261

I had to admit he was right. We needed to get rid of Carlton. Once I got him to shoot Carlton, I could put his ass in jail or kill him myself.

"Well, the dead man is walking, and he needs my help. But what makes you think I am going to help you?" I asked, smirking.

"We both know it's the only way to keep Alexis and MY BABY safe."

That smug ass nigger thought he was going to come in my house and remind me that he fucked my wife and got her pregnant. *I may not kill him, but tonight, I am going to kick his ass,* I thought as I sat the gun down on the end table and charged at Wesley. Just as I was close to him, he stepped to the side, and I crashed into the wall then fell to the floor. *Stupid ass move, Chase!* I scolded myself as Wesley's big ass boot connected to my chest, and I gasped for air.

"STOP!" screamed Alexis, keeping Wesley from stomping me again. Wesley walked over to her and placed his arms around her while I struggled to catch my breath.

He held her as she fussed. While he was distracted with her, I got up and picked up my phone. I texted Carlton and told him to come to me. It was time to get rid of both of these Black bastards.

Carlton

My mouth dropped to the floor when I had a personal greeting from Afon. He just strolled into my house like he was the king of the fucking castle. Then, he sat down at my desk. *What the fuck is happening here?* I asked myself as I sat in the small chair in front of the desk.

"To what do I owe this surprise?"

"Elle no longer wishes to work with you, so that means that you have a problem."

"That BITCH," I blurted out. "What the fuck am I supposed to do?" I asked.

"You better make it right and fast. This is fucking with my money," he stated calmly then got up, heading to the door. Before he left, he said I had forty-eight hours.

The door slammed behind him. *What the fuck?* Just as I thought the words, my phone started to chime. I got a text from a random number. It was from Chase. He must be ready to watch me fuck his bitch. Then, I was going to cut her fucking throat.

I texted my right hand, Tony, and told him to bring backup. We had a cracker to kill.

I needed one of those son of a bitch to make sure Camille was dead too.

Alexis

Seeing Wesley made my night. God knew I missed the hell out of his ass. Him just showing up at the house had me nervous as fuck. It seemed as if he was looking for a fight. My heart damn near jumped out as they started to fight. In all fairness, Chase needed his ass beat. He thought he was untouchable. Well, he learned today. If I didn't think Wes would have killed him, I would have let them fight. But I screamed who knows what, and Wes stopped. He rushed over to me and hugged me tight and whispered, "Get out of here. Don't fight me on this. Just get your ass out of here right now!"

While debating on if I should fight Wesley or not, Chase picked up his phone.

"Come with me, babe. Please! I have a horrible feeling."

"Alexis, trust me and do as I say. Okay?"

His tone was urgent and scary, so the only choice I had was to leave out the house. Grabbing Chase's keys, I noticed that there were two men sitting in a dark blue car. Wesley had me fucked up if he thought I was just going to leave. Slowly making my way to Chase's car, I unlocked the door, got in, closed the door, and tried to remember where

Chase kept a 9mm under the driver side seat. Pulling the keys out my purse and turning the car on, I backed it up a little to make it seem as if I was leaving. I had no plans on leaving Wes. That could have been throwing his ass to the wolves.

After sitting two houses down, I saw Carlton's ass pull up, and something inside me snapped. He parked his car and had his goons stand outside the house. I called Wesley, and as soon as he answered, I told him how many men were out there and that it looked like there was going to be trouble.

His reply was, "I am good," but I did not trust that shit. I had to think of a way to get in the house without the men grabbing my ass. "Let me see how good my drive by skills are," I thought out loud. First, I needed to see how many guns were in this car.

Hopping out the car, I made my way to the trunk. Lo and behold, this worthless son of a bitch only had a damn gym bag. So, that left me with one gun and only the bullets that were in the chamber. I couldn't call the cops because they were all friends with Chase. What the fuck was I supposed to do?

In all reality, no one was going to expect me to have a gun in my purse. Getting back in the car, something said to look under the passenger seat. There was one more little gun. God was shining on my stupid ass today.

The number one lesson I had learned from Chase was that I needed to observe the scene and then make my move. I drove to the store and bought some small smoke bombs. Everyone needed to have a plan, and I had mine all figured out.

Wesley

Damn, I had missed Alexis's ass so much, and it brought joy to my heart knowing that I was about to have her all to myself without her punk ass husband getting in the way. He was so lucky that she stopped me from beating the life out of his punk ass. Now, it was him and I sitting in his living room, trying to see who was going to bust a move first.

Twenty minutes later, we were still looking at each other like dumb and dumber as the door opened. In strolled three men that I had never seen before. They had their guns in hand, pointed at me. I was not sure at this point if my crew would get here in enough time, and a nigga was feeling a little worried. No one was saying a word, and guns were out. There was no need for me to pull my weapon at this time. I would be fighting a losing battle.

"What are we going to do with this nigger?" one of the guys asked Chase.

"We are waiting on his punk ass cousin to get here, then we are going to kill them both," he calmly replied.

A few moments later, the door flew open and in came Carlton, Chris, and Big Tony. I felt a little better.

"The dead has risen. Fool, your ass ain't Jesus. Why the fuck are you standing here?" Carlton asked.

He had a punk ass smirk on his face. I couldn't wait to shoot this son of a bitch. I mean, I wanted to shoot him and fuck my baby in his blood. Okay, that may be a little sick.

"Well, boys, it looks as if y'all have some unfinished business. I think I will give you a few moments to work out your issues, then I'ma kill both of you," Chase stated.

Chase and the first three guys left the room. That left Carlton, me, Chris, Big Tony, a dude name Mal, and some new cat. Mal looked at me and then to Carlton and decided that he didn't want to pick sides, so he went to guard the door.

Chris and Big Tony turned their guns to Carlton. The odds were now in my favor. A cheesy grin came across my face. "Do you have any last words, Carlton?"

He burst into laughter then looked at me and said, "Yes, it felt so good ramming my dick in your bitch, cumming all over your baby's head."

That was the point of no control.

Before he could finish talking shit, he was being choked and slammed into the ground. He was going to die, but first, he had to learn a lesson. While Carlton was on the ground, I kicked him a few times, and I realized that he wasn't fighting back. He must be planning to shoot me. Taking my foot and kicking him in the head, forcing him to grab at his face, allowed me to keep track of his hands. He couldn't shoot me and protect his grill at the same time.

I heard Alexis scream. *I am going to kill her ass*, I thought, turning my attention towards the door.

Chase had her by the arm. A part of me knew that he would not hurt her, but her silly ass would jump in front of a bullet to save me. *Fuck*, I said in my head.

"Alexis, I told you to get the fuck out of here," I screamed at her.

She smiled at me and snatched away from Chase. Shit was about to get out of hand. I could tell as a horrible feeling came in my gut. Seconds later, the house started to fill up with smoke.

What the fuck was going on?

EPILOGUE

Chase

It was taking them niggers way too long to kill each other. I decided to go help them when I saw Alexis's ass peeping in the window. Rushing outside, I yoked her up by the arm. She let out a horrible scream. I hoped that I hurt her stupid ass. This mess was all her fault.

"Hello, my sweet. I want you to witness this mess you started. All you had to do was be faithful. But no! You had to fuck your past."

"Chase, you fucked that stripper, so who are you to point fingers? You got the bitch pregnant," she shot back at me.

"I took care of that problem. Camille will never bother us again. Meanwhile, I get to raise Wesley's child," I whispered, forcing her in the room. It looked like I acted too soon because Wes was beating the shit out of Carlton. Once he laid eyes on Alexis, he stopped, and she snatched away from me. My eyes started burning as the house filled with colorful smoke, and the lights went out. They had to throw about two hundred of them because the smoke was thick, and it was hard to see.

I heard someone say, "Good night, bitches." Then, shots were fired, and I heard Alexis scream.

Alexis

Carlton pulled his gun and started to fire. It scared me, and I let out a scream. I dropped to the floor because Carlton was out for blood. Wesley got in front of me to block the shots from hitting me. There was a gun on the floor under the couch. It was a good thing that Wesley had been teaching me how to shot because I grabbed the gun and started to shot with Wesley. A few seconds later, and everyone was shot but Wesley and I. We were the last two standing when Chase came in the house.

"Alexis, I can get you out of this. All you have to do is leave Wesley and come home to me."

Before I could even reply, Wesley let out two rounds. One hit Chase in the head; the other hit the wall. My heart stopped. I loved Chase, but I knew that this would have ended badly.

"Alexis, let's get the fuck out of here."

The End

Made in the USA
Las Vegas, NV
20 May 2022

49139562R00154